Deadly Glance

Dallas Taylor

Praise for Deadly Glance

I read this book in two sittings, as it was very difficult to put down - a real page-turner. The story pulls you in immediately with the main character, Jeff, and his two law partners, Bob and Lil, who have an up and coming law practice specializing in trade matters and government affairs. The plot moves quickly and keeps you on the edge of your seat. Anyone who loves a good mystery will not be disappointed in this book. I am must hoping there will be a sequel. Move over John Grisham!!!

Margaret B.

Dallas Taylor's Book Deadly Glance is an excellent read. Smart character development, rich plot and enough twists and turns that make it hard to put down. Move over Connelly and Turow, Taylor is taking her rightful spot in the Legal thriller world!

AS

Deadly Glance

Dallas Taylor

To

My friends and family who have supported me and inspired me to keep writing so I could realize a dream. To my editor who guided me through the process so expertly and patiently, thank you. My muses and coaches and angels along the way who have reminded me to keep pushing, dreaming and achieving.

Prologue

Jeff sat quietly on his cold leather couch, staring out the window. He could see cars driving slowly by, taking their passengers leisurely through their lives. The lights from the cars danced through the trees, casting shadows over his living room and making it come alive with the ghosts that haunted his thoughts. He stared blankly ahead, his thoughts turning involuntarily to her.

He realized now, of course, that he might never know. Everything he had seen of her had vanished into the night, as suddenly as the day she had appeared. On that day, he'd known immediately that he had to help her. His insight could read deeper than the surface of her smile. Perhaps it was in the tilt of her smile, or the blankness of her eyes. She was in trouble. It was subtle, but it was there.

It had all started with a simple game of cards ... Hearts, he remembered. He had decided on a Tuesday to wander into another world as a distraction from his normal routine of working late at the office. And there she was, catching his glance from across the room. *Who is she?* he'd wondered to himself. The thought caught at his breath, and his eyes had devoured her as she flirtatiously batted her eyes around the room in sheer defiance of the kind of attention it garnered. She absolutely lit the place up. Yet there it was ... something in her look ... something that looked like fear.

Jeff had watched intently as a smartly dressed man in a gray double-breasted suit, elegantly wearing his wealth, whispered something to her. She had looked up at Jeff as the other man finished, and their eyes had locked. Jeff had tried quickly to regain his composure at that point, and began to look at a waiter behind her. He'd known, though, that he had been caught staring. His trained eye told him that something was out of place. It was subtle, but it was there. Perhaps it was that the men around her appeared displaced in this casual bar.

The man in gray, still leaning closely over her, had looked at Jeff as well, smiling slyly and sliding his fingers slowly through his slicked-back black locks. The lights in the club glistened on each shiny strand as he shifted his hair away from his face, Jeff remembered. His ring sparkled in the light – diamonds visible from across the smoky room. His chiseled features would have probably intimidated most men, but Jeff found the challenge rather passé. He had experienced his own success with women, mostly because of his pure love and sense of enjoyment. He met the eyes of the man leaning close to the beautiful woman, and took his measure in an instant. Yes, he was part of it, Jeff thought. This man was part of the something that was not quite right.

He took his eyes off the man and glanced back at the woman, catching her eyes again and grinning. She smiled back, but it was a distant smile ... and it left as soon as it came.

Jeff suddenly realized he was half a hand into his card game, and turned his attention back to the cards, grabbing for his glass and glancing at his cards to see if he should fold. By the time he looked back in her direction, she was gone, and so was his card game. *Damn it*, he thought.

He had returned to the club several times over the next several weeks, hoping to see her again. He enjoyed the distraction from his everyday life, and the crowd watching was second to none.

He wondered each time if he'd catch sight of the gorgeous blonde again. Something about her was a piece to a puzzle that had intrigued him, and the slight but nagging feeling that she was in danger stuck with him. His past trained him to always calculate and measure. He knew how to read a man by his body language, his smile, the way he held himself. And the men that surrounded the blonde in this club made him instinctively nervous. This beautiful woman was keeping company with the wrong crowd, and he wanted to know why.

He didn't know why he was so interested, and he knew it was none of his business, really. He wasn't ready for a relationship at this point in his life.

Jeff didn't like to think of himself as shallow, but he knew he could have any woman he wanted. His looks were engaging, his charm stemming from his confidence and deep, dark eyes. Yet he had given his heart away a long time ago, and he wasn't sure if he would ever be ready to give it again. He poured himself into his work instead, seeking escape from the pain he'd found in love.

He held his 6'2" stature in a cool and casual style, and had an athletic build built on years of sports – he had never lifted a weight in all of his thirty-nine years, but he had played baseball since childhood. One of his few memories with his dad was playing catch in the back yard. He continued playing as he grew older, going on to be a star pitcher with the University of Texas during his undergraduate years. He played minor league ball with the Durham Bulls, but also decided to get his law degree at University of North Carolina at the same time. His life had taken a sharp turn, then, when he was recruited into the clandestine operations for first the NSA then the CIA. He worked with those operations for a total of eight years; a fact well concealed from his current clientele. When he returned to civilian life, he played one year in the majors at the Texas Rangers before hanging up his jersey for his law practice, and for Sidney.

These days, he kept his body well toned with frequent basketball games against the boys from neighboring law firms. He'd also started a baseball league for the lawyers in town, and played every weekend. He was a ringer, and the women appreciated it.

He worked hard to treat the women he met well, and won them over with both his body and his mind. He looked at each and every woman with his deep, mesmerizing brown eyes, and extended a pure appreciation to each. Yet the blonde held his attention more than any other had. A single glance suspended a moment in time, emblazoned forever in his memory. He hadn't noticed a woman in this way since Sidney had captured his heart in college.

That relationship hadn't ended well, and he lost a piece of himself in the aftermath. These days, he shared his heart with very few, having locked it safely away since that fateful day. Now it beat a bit harder; perhaps it was asking to be let out of the box, at last. Perhaps, a glimmer of hope.

Chapter 1

By the third week, Jeff had found a familiar and comfortable table near the bar. He was also getting to know the local crowd. Run by some new lawyers in town, the Hearts game he'd joined was a way for colleagues to mingle, and had become quite popular with the jet set crowd. These days, it went well beyond the lawyers that had started it.

Jeff found himself instinctively scanning the room for familiar faces, strange occurences and things out of place. He found he couldn't abandon his clandestine training for long. The blonde woman and her male entourage were intriguing. He knew there was more to the story, and he found he loved the game of Hearts. So what was the harm in a little private eye work on the side? He had been burying himself in his cases for the last several years, and his friend Holly had been prodding him to find a hobby ... anything to start having fun again. This seemed to do the trick.

He'd decided to bring company this time, his long-time friend Holly, and had convinced her to see his new game and perhaps meet some new people. Holly had been friends with Jeff for many years, originally meeting him through his wife Sidney. Holly and Sidney had been best friends.

"I thought you didn't like to play cards," Jeff said as they walked up Main toward the club.

"I thought you never won at this game," she jabbed back. They were strolling slowly, confidently yet playfully prodding and teasing each other as they walked off their dinner.

"Hey, did you come to have a good time tonight, or are you just here to give me a hard time?" he asked suddenly.

"Good time of course, which may include some ribbing here and there, you know me!" she responded with a smile.

"Well, ok. Go easy on me, I'm vulnerable," Jeff said quietly. He grabbed his heart and smiled. "Well, now, show me your stuff Miss Holly Darling. Show me how it's done. Care for a little wager?"

"Kiss your money goodbye, Mr. Walker, kiss it goodbye."

Jeff laughed as they walked into the club. They spotted a rowdy table to the right of the bar, filled with animated smiles and flailing arms – sure signs of winning.

"Hey, save that table over there, Holly," Jeff said, pointing to the now-familiar table. "I'll grab some starter drinks. What do you want?" He instinctively scanned the room as he talked, knowing from experience that this table provided a good view of the entire room, and saw that his familiar seat – the one with the best view – was left empty, as if the others already knew it was his.

The Hearts game started by the original lawyers had grown to take over much of the club, with most of the tables dedicated to the game until 9 p.m., when the club converted back to a dance and music joint. They had several tables to choose from, but Jeff had become partial to his regular table.

"Ok," Holly responded, walking straight to the table.

"I'll get the drinks," Jeff shouted after her. He turned toward the bar, leaving Holly to find the table.

Holly didn't hesitate, and left Jeff to scan the room. Eyes throughout the room turned to catch a glance as she enchantingly stepped across the room, smiling at anyone who looked at her. Her spirit and vitality brightened any room and any face. She turned to wave at Jeff when she arrived at the two open seats at his claimed table. Seeing that she had found their seats, he turned toward the bar and found a familiar bar stool.

The bartender looked up and smiled. "Hey, Jeff, haven't seen you for a couple of days. How are things?"

Jeff knew that being on a first-name basis with the bartender was a sign that his clandestine efforts had been blown, but he ignored it for the moment. He'd worked hard to avoid notice in the bar, so that he could do research on the beautiful woman, but the bartender's use of his first name indicated he had failed. He still enjoyed the scene.

"Not bad. Still searching for the real thing," he shouted, projecting his voice above the band next to the bar.

"Hey about the woman you're with ... she's not bad. You know, if you don't want her..." The bartender's voice trailed off as Jeff scanned the room for faces he knew.

"She can speak for herself. You'll have to ask her," Jeff responded, knowing full well that Holly would decide on her own though he wondered if this guy was the right guy.

"Hey Jack, how about a 7&7 and a martini?" The bartender raised an eyebrow and quickly went to work on the drinks. In the back of the club on stage, Jeff spotted a familiar face that he hadn't seen in a while. He let his eyes scan the length of her body, taking in the long, skin-tight gown, and finally coming to rest on her exquisite face. She looked up and caught his eyes on her, and he smiled.

He was still looking at the blonde on the stage, searching again for her accomplices – who were nowhere to be found – when he caught Holly's movement out of the corner of his eye and turned to greet her.

She grabbed his arm, asking, "What's taking so long?" She didn't want for a response, but pulled him along to guide him to the tables. "I've got two great seats back at your table, Jeff."

She led him back to their seats, and he saw that the couples at the table were already waving at her. He glanced back to the stage but quickly turned his attention to his best friend and the table of new friends. She was a quick wit, and could have been a great litigator. She also read people quickly and knew who to get to know and who to keep at arm's length. Her ability to read people so well had led him to hire her a few times to help with jury selection, which had become such an art form. And she never turned that particular skill off; she used it every day, on everyone she met. Apparently that meant that this table was full of people to her liking.

In addition to being a great reader of people, she had a brilliant, engaging personality, and a smile that wouldn't stop. Her bright nature and infectious grin combined for an effect that no stranger could resist.

"And this is my good-looking date, Jeff," she told them, continuing a conversation she'd already started. The others nodded in welcome. Holly also had a great memory, and she called out each person's name at the table, in turn. Jeff shook each hand as she called out their names. Finally she neared the last person sitting to their right.

"And this is Milt," she said. "He runs the steel manufacturing plant south of the city."

Jeff and Holly took their seats facing the stage and settled in.

***

The next few hours were amazing. Jeff was winning every single hand, and before the night was over he had won over $5,000. He knew having Holly there kept him a little more alert, a little more competitive, and a little sharper. He'd also been getting better and better at the game, with increased focus. He was moving toward being very good at Hearts.

At the end of the night, Holly waited for Jeff to collect his winnings from the table and finish shaking hands with the other players. They were all agreeing to meet back there in a week for another fun evening when Jeff noticed that the blonde had now left the stage and was walking directly toward them. He looked to Holly and was pleasantly surprised.

Holly's face lit up again as she saw the woman from the stage, and she waved. The other woman recognized her immediately, and her face broke out in an answering smile.

"Holly, my God, how are you? How long has it been? Years, isn't it?"

Jeff watched and listened to her voice; it was just as she had sounded while singing – sultry, with an airy quality about it. She still appeared to be hiding something, but it was slight. She walked confidently, moving gracefully across the room, yet her eyes betrayed her, nervously scanning the room, watching for someone and defensive in case that person may appear.

Jeff watched, drawn to her so intently he was nearly obsessed with her and her story.

Holly nodded, pleased and surprised at the woman's memory. "Victoria, it's good to see you. How long have you been singing here?" she asked. She had noticed Jeff staring, and now smiled and winked at him. He looked slowly from one woman to the other, awed.

"Well I just started tonight, actually," Victoria answered. "I was here a few months ago to talk to the owners, and they asked me to become one of the regular acts. I really had to scramble to get a band together, because I haven't sung in quite a while. Nasty divorce, nightmare legal fees ... but you don't want to hear about that." She sighed and shrugged in resignation, then turned toward Jeff.

Holly didn't miss the transition, and turned to Jeff as well. "Victoria, this is my good friend Jeff."

"Victoria," Jeff said, casually taking her hand and kissing it. "It's a pleasure." He smiled up into her eyes, wondering ... and there it was again, that frightened glance to the side. He looked for her thug-like entourage, wondering who she was so scared of, but she was alone.

"Oh my," Victoria said, clearly impressed. "What a gentleman." She gave him a large smile, and then grew serious. "You look familiar. Do I know you? Hey you're a lawyer in town, right? I'm pretty sure I saw you in the news."

Holly gave Jeff a darting glance, then looked back at Victoria. She frowned in warning. "Yes, Jeff gets his share of air time. That's true," she led. Holly watched the two standing before her for a moment and then turned toward the bar. Victoria, would you – or you, Jeff – like something from the bar? I need to stretch my legs. I've been sitting here watching Jeff rack up for the past hour."

Jeff nodded, smiling at her ability to take a hint. "Certainly. What would you like, Victoria? It's my treat, absolutely." He noticed his calculating demeanor beginning to dissolve; his courtroom front began to fade, and sighed to himself. Yes, he was definitely more interested in this woman than he'd allowed himself to realize. He couldn't take his eyes off of her, and his fingers were dying to run themselves along her arms. He felt as though he was leaning into her, as well. Holly noted too, and told Jeff later, that for a moment they looked as if they were old acquaintances, getting to know each other again.

At the mention of the drinks, he and Victoria progressed through an awkward yet almost undetectable pause.

Finally she shook her head and held up one hand, refusing the drink. "I'm sorry, I really can't stay to visit. I need to get back for the next set." All three looked back to the stage, where they saw the rest of the band searching anxiously for their singer. They looked lost without her, and Jeff and Holly nodded.

"I'll take a rain check, though." Victoria slanted her eyes toward Jeff, reading him, and turned back to Holly. "It was great to see you again, Holly. Next time you want to come to the Brooklyn, let me know and I'll get you on the guest list if I'm singing."

She hugged Holly quickly and turned back to find the rest of her band members. By the time she had reached the stage, the band was already beginning a syncopated beat. The music incited the crowd to spontaneous clapping, and couples began heading for the dance floor. The songstress quickly picked up the cue, grabbed the mike, and belted out a smooth note. The entire audience turned to focus on her.

Jeff watched closely as Victoria took the stage, and caught her eye again as she turned in their direction. Neither broke the eye contact until Victoria closed her eyes to finish the long note she was holding.

***

Holly took a moment to soak it all in. Jeff had obviously taken a liking to Victoria, with the way he was gazing after her, and she wondered how long this had been going on. She hadn't seen a woman catch his attention since Sidney. Holly and Sidney had been best friends, and Sidney had introduced Holly to Jeff himself. They'd been married for five years. Both successful, both bright and shining in their careers, they'd talked about having children, and everything had seemed perfect.

Then one day, Sidney mysteriously disappeared, with no explanation.

Sidney and Jeff had been soul mates, however, and even in her absence, Holly didn't think he'd ever been truly over her. Away from the watchful eyes of his friends, family and colleagues, she knew that he still cried at night, remembering her sleeping next time him. He had confessed it to her on numerous occasions, though she'd never known what to say. She had thought at the time that the only way to truly get on with his life was to leave Sidney in the past. At her urging, he had finally slipped his wedding ring off and stuck it in his sock drawer.

While she had encouraged him to come to terms with the fact that he would probably never see Sidney again, and to try to move on, she'd been both relieved and somewhat sorry to see that the ring was gone.

Jeff hadn't mentioned her name in months.

Perhaps his connection with Victoria was a good turn of fate, Holly thought to herself. He seemed happier. She glanced again at Victoria on the stage, but decided that it was time to go.

"Well, that was fun," she said suddenly. She turned to him, grabbing his arm to get his attention. "What do you want from the bar?"

"Tell Jack I'll have the usual," he answered, his eyes still on Victoria.

"You know the bartender?" she asked, surprised. She frowned at him, wondering. "This is worse than I thought –

you really *have* blown your cover." She tossed her sun-highlighted red hair in frustration and headed purposefully toward the bar.

Jeff turned to watch her walk away, and noted the other men following her with their eyes. Holly knew him well indeed; he'd shared with her that he was casually investigating the thugs running the bar and who appeared to be with Victoria, but she hadn't realized the extent of his visits there.

***

Jeff searched the room and noticed couples flirting and laughing at the tables around him. His eyes moved again to the bar, where Holly was receiving a good deal of attention from the eager bartender. The middle-aged, single, and married women who had been receiving his attention all night looked on, obviously irritated by being upstaged, and threw their money on the bar. Jeff laughed; he had known Holly for a long time, and while she was very attractive, he knew that she would always be his wife's best friend – and his friend – and nothing more. That was a line he would never cross. Holly wouldn't either, he knew. And it was this unspoken line that had led them to such an amazing friendship. No one else understood how they could be so close without being romantic, but they didn't care; it was their friendship, and wasn't for anyone else to understand.

While Jeff has been thinking about their relationship, Holly herself appeared, her voice in his ear snapping him back into the present.

"Well, you made $5,000 and I have a date with Jack next Saturday night. So I suppose this night counts as a success."

She'd returned with their two drinks, and they walked over to sit on a couch near the table where they had played cards. The card players at the table were dispersing now, and the club was transitioning from social games to nightclub. Holly and Jeff sipped their drinks and watched the change quietly.

Finally, Holly said, "You seem happier, Jeff."

Jeff nodded in silence, not knowing what she expected him to say. He thought about her words. He found himself reflecting less on the past and becoming more excited about the future. This new woman who had intrigued him seemed to bring him more to the present. He reflected for a moment about Sidney and felt a familiar, yet lessened, pang of sadness for the loss. He knew it was time to move on.

"It's been a long time, and moving on doesn't mean you've forgotten," Holly continued.

"I know, Holly, I know."

He looked down at his hand and realized that Holly had probably noticed the ring was gone. Yes, it was time. But he knew he still needed some time, and really didn't feel like talking about it. He stood in silence for a moment and Holly seemed to understand. Finally her voice broke him out of his thought.

"It was a fun night, Jeff. Thank you for bringing me here." She beamed, then reached over and lightly squeezed her good friend's arm.

He smiled back. "Atta girl." She'd had her rough patches in relationships over the past couple of years, and he was happy to see her interested in dating again.

They sat in silence for a moment.

"You know," Holly added suddenly, "things look like they're turning up, Jeff. Things are turning up."

He knew she hadn't dated in the years, since a terrible incident with her ex-boyfriend, in which she nearly lost her life. He had seen her in her lowest moments and had watched her gain strength and conviction in these past years and months.

"I think this is turning out to be a very good year Holly, a very good year," Jeff said, grabbing her hand. "Why don't we split this joint, go home, and do it all over again tomorrow?"

"Well if we don't they are going to kick us out of here anyway!" she exclaimed.

"Yes, ma'am, this place is about to turn into a zoo." They looked toward the door, where a line of young men and women were lining up, waiting impatiently for the club to turn into the late-night dance club. "Yep, definitely not our scene."

They turned their attention back on to the band, who were packing up their instruments, preparing for the disco ball and DJ to take over the stage.

Jeff stood and held his arm out dramatically for Holly to grab, so that he could lead her out of the bar. She smiled and stood obligingly, taking his arm and allowing him to accompany her towards the door. She waved at a few of their new friends leaving the club.

As they walked out the door, the night air hit them with refreshing coolness, and Jeff looked up at the bright sky above them. He could actually see some stars, which were typically very hard to see against the bright skyline of the city. He made a note of this moment because he felt really good, and realized that he couldn't recall the last time he'd felt this alive. He paused and self-consciously reached for the ring that was no longer on his finger. It was time … it was definitely time to move on.

After walking for a few minutes, they found his car tucked under a lamp post, just where they had left it. He opened Holly's door and then walked over to the driver's side, slid into the driver's seat and pushed the start button. The car roared to life and they started their twenty-minute drive back to Holly's.

Jeff watched Holly walk up the driveway and disappear around the garage on the walk to her front door. He sat for a moment and waited until the dimly lit house brightened. She always went through the house, turning on the lights room by room to illuminate the entire place. It was something she'd learned to do as a child, he knew, when she'd been left alone often, and terrified of the dark. He smiled to himself at the thought, and then let his mind drift to the events of the evening.

Victoria was no longer a mystery, and that alone had made the night worthwhile. Now that he'd seen her without the thugs that surrounded her the first night he laid eyes on her, she seemed much softer. There was something about her that was drawing him closer ... he knew that he was letting his guard down, though he shouldn't be. He couldn't help it, though he was looking at her less as the subject of his curiosity about the company she kept and more as a woman he wanted to see again, for his own personal reasons.

"Damn," he said suddenly, interrupting his own revere. He'd promised his business partner that he would call, and forgotten, until he thought of his own investigation.

He grabbed the phone out of his glove compartment and punched the numbers in. Something caught his eye before he finished, though, and he glanced at the passenger-side window. Nothing. Just blackness. Was it a reflection that caught his eye? Sitting in Holly's driveway, with no protection in the dead of night, he began to feel anxious, and decided to check his messages later.

He put the car into reverse, and then paused. He was sure he'd seen movement, this time. There, just behind the tree in Holly's front yard.

"No way," he said quietly, straining his eyes toward the tree. "Just my imagination." The sound of his voice cleared the cobwebs from his head, and he threw the phone into the passenger seat. Whatever was out there, he was going to check it out before he left.

He put the car back in park, grabbed the gun from under his seat – loaded of course – and slowly opened the door. Moving quietly, he stepped smoothly out of the car and onto the concrete driveway, and then listened closely. He held the gun casually by his right side, fingering the side of the trigger, and started walking. By the time he reached the opposite side of the car, his eyes had adjusted to the dark night and he could see several bushes lining the driveway, moving quietly in a light breeze. He pushed away the brush with the hand holding the loaded gun, to look behind it. Through the opening he could see only the neighbors' fence. Nothing. He took a deep breath and decided not to say anything to Holly, as it was all clear.

Turning, he took a quick walk along the side of the house and still found nothing suspicious. He walked slowly back to the car, still scanning the driveway and street to make sure he hadn't missed anything.

Satisfied, he stepped back into his car, pulled the door shut, pushed the gun back under the seat, threw the car in reverse and pulled out of the driveway. As he settled into the monotony of driving, his mind journeyed through the events of the evening. He drove on autopilot, navigating the familiar thirty-minute drive through instinct and memory.

Victoria reminded him of Sidney, he thought, and in a good way. It was a feeling he'd had when he was with Sidney, that leaning-in feeling. When he was with Sidney he felt whole, and that he could lean into her and that it was safe. He felt that line where two people become more like one, complimenting each other in a way that made you feel like you'd arrived home. When he was around Victoria he was reminded of that feeling and the last time he'd felt it.

He thought about their last weekend together, and sighed; they had driven down to the beach, where friends of theirs had a beach house. They'd taken their dog Tucker, an affable blonde lab that bounded with joy and was loyal to his family. The dog had nuzzled his way into a blanket in the back seat of their 1994 Toyota Forerunner, and he and Sidney had set off. He remembered reaching out to grab her hand, and holding it through the trip. He could still smell her perfume.

They were celebrating at the time; he had just won his first big case, and they'd used it as an excuse for a vacation. They were starting a life together and everything looked so bright. It was the beginning of something great, and he knew everything was going to be wonderful forever.

When he pulled into his own driveway, he stared at the house, surprised. All of the lights in the house were blazing, and the glow extended out over the lawn and driveway. He frowned; he never turned the lights on before he left the house, and he knew for a fact that he hadn't done so tonight.

The lights on and other things that seemed slightly off tonight added to his discomfort. His instincts were telling him to beware, but he wasn't quite sure why.

Since leaving the club, he'd had a sensation of things being slightly off. He had learned from his training that this feeling was not something to ignore, and he paused, but then shook himself. These weren't CIA operations, he reminded himself. This was him getting home after a night out with a friend. Better to be cautious, though, than be sorry.

He reached back under his seat and once again carefully pulled out his SigSauer, then sat in his driveway, car still running, considering his options. He could pull into his garage or quietly turn off his engine, leaving the car parked in the driveway. This could provide him with an element of surprise if someone was indeed lurking in his house, an uninvited guest. It would also give him more room to maneuver.

His eyes scanned the house again, looking for any signs, but he found everything to be as it had always been. The house was nestled quietly on the lake, surrounded by lush, swaying trees. The night still black, but the streetlights were brighter in his neighborhood than Holly's, and that provided him good visibility to check around the house.

He pulled into the garage and turned off the car, then headed straight for the back door, entering cautiously, gun in his hand. He glanced around the room and then out the windows to the back yard, which was brightly lit from the full moon. Nothing suspicious there. He slid quietly through the house, checking every room with his heart pounding, but found everything to be as he had left it – a mess. The laundry spilled over the living room furniture, and the dirty dishes in the kitchen sink looked like they had multiplied, as most dirty dishes do.

"Ah, the comforts of home." He smiled in satisfaction, admiring his mess. It wasn't tidy, but it was his, and it comforted him to see it undisturbed. He didn't know what he'd been expecting, but the sight of his dirty laundry and mess made him think that his imagination had been playing tricks on him; everything was as it should be. He must have left the lights on. It was the only explanation.

He shed his Italian leather shoes in the tile entryway and walked gently over the cool walkway. His feet met the soft plush carpet as he continued to drape his clothing, piece by piece, across anything in his way. By the time he reached his bed upstairs, he was wearing only his silk boxers, and sank into his bed and drifted quickly off to sleep.

Chapter 2

Bob hit the end button on his phone and ground his teeth. Where on earth could he be? He'd been trying to get in touch with his law partner Jeff for over an hour now, with no luck, and it made him incredibly nervous. What had happened? Was he in trouble? Had he lost his way somewhere? Had he been ... Bob swallowed hard ... killed? He began to pace across his den again, as he had done for the past hour, stopping only long enough to look at the phone and dial his partner once again.

"Think, think," he said to himself, listening to the phone ring on the other end and go to voicemail.

"What the hell? Jesus, what's happened?" he asked, his mind racing. He didn't expect an answer; he'd been leaving the same message, in different variations, for hours, and the pacing and stress were now causing him to sweat.

His own phone rang at 9:00 pm. If only he hadn't picked up, he thought now. If only he'd let it go to voicemail, the way his gut had told him to. But he'd picked up, and it had been another threat. Bob and his partner had been receiving threats for over a month now about a bill they were supporting regarding affirmative action, and Bob was beginning to think that he was the only one taking the threats seriously. It didn't make sense that anyone would take offense to an affirmative action bill, at least not enough to make it lethal. Generally the partners of the firm agreed that calls like these were simply an annoyance, likely from some pranksters in college, bored of their normal activities. These calls felt different, though, and Bob had begun to panic.

Jeff Walker and Bob Wright started their law firm – Walker, Wright and Turner – with Lil Turner several years before, and neither had experienced threats such as these.

Jeff had tried to calm Bob down, telling him that the threats meant nothing. But Bob had reached the edge. It was easy for Jeff to say that when Bob was the only one receiving the calls. Why had they singled him out? How was it that Jeff could blow off the threats to his life? And were the threats as dangerous – and real – as Bob feared? He turned sharply at the thought and began to pace to the other side of the room.

Their firm had gotten their fair share of prank calls, mysterious notes, and prank packages in the mail. Most all of them ended in a police investigation, but each was investigated quickly and relegated to the equivalent of a college prank.

The local college activists had, on occasion, set up picket lines when they decided they didn't like one of Walker, Wright, and Turner's clients. But the protests had always been friendly, small in size, and disbanded within hours. That was college students trying to make a statement, and show their own importance. This felt different. This felt dangerous.

He started to dial the police again.

***

"Chief Kouros here," the officer barked into the receiver. He was sitting at the front desk of the police station, the man in charge of the phones for the day. *Never fails*, he thought. As soon as he was about to run home to be with the wife and kids, and have a decent meal, the phone started ringing.

"Hey Lou, it's Bob. I keep getting the same damn phone calls I was telling you about."

Bob sounded agitated, and Chief Kouros could hear him pacing. He sighed. This wasn't the first time the man had called, but there was no new information.

"Calm down, Bob. I'm sure it's just another one of those prank calls. We get hundreds of calls about these every day, and they hardly ever amount to anything." The chief thought about the hot pot roast his wife had told him she was cooking tonight, and his mouth began to water. If this man would stop calling, he thought, he could go home to a hot meal and his family.

"Hardly ever? What happens when they do?" Bob didn't pause long enough to let Kouros answer. "I just got another one two minutes ago. I've been pacing like an animal, and I can't get a hold of my partner. I've tried, repeatedly, but he's not answering his phone either. What if something's

31

happened to him? What if we're both in danger? This whole thing's got to stop. Jesus."

"Calm down," the officer answered. "Listen, I'll send a patrol car out there and have them drive by on the hour tonight. They'll keep an eye on you. Listen, Bob, these pranks happen all the time. I'm sure it's nothing." Kouros paused and added, "But if it *is* something, we'll get to the bottom of it."

"I sure hope you're right. And thanks." Chief Kouros waited a moment, listening to Bob's breathing on the other end of the line, and the man continued. "I think this may be connected to a case I've been working. These calls picked up about the time we got this case. And I don't think these guys mess around, Kouros."

"We'll send a guy out there right now, Bob, stay alert," Kouros added. He hung up the phone, and then turned to another officer. "Hey, send a guy out to patrol Travis Street – here's the address." He jotted an address down on a piece of paper and handed it to the officer. "He's getting some threatening phone calls and he's pretty spooked. Thinks it has to do with one of his cases. Get the officer to take his statement first, then patrol on the hour."

"You got it, boss."

Chapter 3

Jeff awoke to a bright, clear morning. His curtains were open and he could see light glistening on his ceiling from the dancing water below his window. He stood up to take in the view, stretching and rubbing the sleep from his eyes.

What a life, he thought, gazing across the view of the lake. The sun rose in the distance, casting its rays across the water. He'd enjoyed the same view every morning for the past ten years, and still couldn't get enough of it. Sighing, he turned from the window and noticed his answering machine blinking. That meant that he had messages. He hadn't noticed the blinking light last night, though the call may have come in after he fell asleep. His thoughts briefly turned back to Victoria's face, and then to Holly and how charming she had been again last night. She was a savior for him.

Then he looked back at the blinking machine and thought about Bob. Maybe that blinking light was a message from him. He and Bob usually talked at least once a day, but yesterday had been the exception. They hadn't spoken last night as they were supposed to, and he wanted to know how the case was coming along.

At that thought, he reached over to hit the play button on the recorder as he passed it on the way to the bathroom. It was old, and clicked loudly while it played the messages, making the voices hard to hear. Jeff's ears had adjusted to the annoying interference, but he reminded himself again to look into upgrading to voicemail. He certainly wasn't up on the latest technology. His attitude had always been one of dealing with it; if the machine worked, why bother replacing it? He had been told by others, though, that he needed to step into the modern world, and he was starting to agree.

"Hey, Bob here," the first message began. "Missed you at the Murphy account dinner tonight. But you didn't avoid much ... just a bunch of the same bullshit. I'll update you at the office tomorrow. Don't forget the Renzi file. Hope you got lucky, buddy. I know I sure got screwed. Those assholes don't know when to quit. See ya."

Jeff loved Bob's tact; he always had such a way with words. He groaned, though; he should have called his partner to check in, or at least save him from the dinner. He'd completely forgotten that they were supposed to make an appearance.

Bob Wright was a man of his word, and was always there for Jeff and Lil. He was the rock in the business and the one everyone always counted on. When something went wrong, everyone turned to Bob to help fix it. When Jeff was running late or missed a meeting, Bob made sure he or someone else was there to fill in and take care of things.

Jeff felt a slight pang of guilt that he'd left Bob alone again to fend for the firm, and missed the meeting entirely. He told himself he wouldn't do it again, although he knew better, given his track record. He'd always make the trial without question, but considered the pre-trial meetings a bunch of BS, and just could never seem to find the time. Thank goodness Bob took care of these things.

The machine clicked again, and the next message began to play. This time it was Holly. "Hey, Romeo, just checking in to see what's cooking. Bye."

She had been charming last night, as usual, and his thoughts began to drift again to the night before, and Holly's part in his new romance. Sometimes he wondered if he and Holly, in another set of circumstances, would have been a good romantic couple. But again, he wouldn't cross that line. He loved her, but when he looked at her he thought of his wife and how they had met. Holly and his wife had known each other in college and become best of friends. When Sidney disappeared, Holly had stood by his side and helped him through everything. She was an understanding and compassionate friend that was always there for him, but that was all it could ever be. And, he thought, they were both happy enough with that relationship.

Suddenly an urgent voice on the recorder snapped him out of his thoughts, and he darted toward the recording to listen more closely.

"Jesus, Jeff, you're not going to believe this. Those assholes are doing it again, and buddy it's really got me spooked. They've already called twice, and it sounds like they mean business. Call me ASAP, buddy. I don't know what to do." Bob sounded more anxious than Jeff had ever heard him, and he swallowed heavily.

His partner had been receiving these calls for a while, and they always spooked him badly. Jeff had tried to calm him down, assuring him they were nothing, but they'd continued. This one had obviously gotten to Bob.

"You're giving them exactly what they want," Jeff said out loud, rehearsing what he'd say to Bob when he got him on the phone. Jeff and Bob both knew that there were indeed bad elements out there, and he was sure there were a few people who wouldn't mind seeing the downfall of Walker, Wright and Turner, but most were unable or unwilling to act on it.

Both Bob and Jeff had been trained by the best – the CIA – to identify, collect and analyze intelligence. The transition into the legal world in the US had been a strange one, but they did see similarities and found their training helpful in reading witnesses, getting information for their cases and such, but so far had never felt that they had to use that intelligence to fend off threats to their own firm.

They had both seen a lot of action during their time in the intelligence business, and both had, for the most part, nerves of steel. Hearing Bob like this made Jeff realize that there was something different about these calls. Bob was spooked, and he wasn't the kind of person that spooked easily. Perhaps he knew more than he was letting on.

He picked the phone up and dialed Bob's number, then waited for Bob to pick up. No answer. He let it ring at least ten times, and slowly pressed the "end" button. Bob had probably already gone to the office, he thought rationally. He glanced at the clock, and saw that it was only 6:30 am. That would be an extraordinarily early Saturday morning, even for Bob, but anything was possible. And what were the alternatives?

Jeff dialed the number again, this time getting Bob's answering service.

He cleared his throat, hoping to sound casual. "Hey, Bob, I got your call last night, buddy. I was out late. Call me or I'll meet you at the office by noon."

He hung up the phone and headed for the shower, tossing his boxers toward the dresser – roughly – and not stopping when he saw them fall to the floor. The entire room was cluttered with trash and laundry, but it made the place home, and made him feel comfortable.

Jeff was so caught up in his thoughts that he didn't hear his own phone start to ring.

Chapter 4

Raul was the best in the business. He had tried to retire many times, but his skill kept him in high demand, and it always seemed to pull him back in ... if the price was right. He knew his own value, and he never worked for less than he was worth. He'd drawn up a schedule of prices once, and stuck to it throughout his career. This job had come out over his standard rate, so he'd jumped at the opportunity. He was already at the chosen spot, and his footsteps were muffled by the soft, matted carpet that lined the musty hallway. The walls had faded to a dusty cream, though a crooked painting on the wall revealed a patch of clean, white paint. *This hotel has seen better days*, Raul thought, coming to his own conclusion about why its tenants had long since departed.

He carried only one non-descript bag, and kept his eyes on the ground. He had spent his entire career learning how to blend into the walls around him, making sure that no one remembered seeing or talking to him, and he put those skills to use today. His assumed name was Joe Schimmer, contractor with Big Town Construction. His papers were in order, and if anyone wanted to call his office to verify his validity, a paid secretary would tell them that he did indeed work for said company. Raul was no novice.

He grabbed the doorknob of the room when he found it, and slipped through the door. The room was empty; only a few rags and cans remained as evidence of prior residents. He spotted a windowsill to the left, propped his bag against it, and opened the top to reveal a plethora of differently sized and colored objects. Raul had this particular equipment memorized, and sang while he began his assembly. He pulled out a standard phone and turned to search the room for a phone jack. He'd done his homework with the local telephone company, and knew that the phone service was still on at the hotel. The owners had closed their doors only one week prior, so everything was dusty, but operational. Very convenient.

"Jackpot," he sang out when he found a jack, snapping the phone cord into place and turning back toward the phone.

He took out of his bag what looked like a small remote control with two cords emerging from it, and plugged one cord into the phone and the other into the wall. It was this device that provided the remote detonation tone to the receiver of the other phone. Everything was simple and straightforward now; the hard part had been breaking into the house earlier, to place the detonator and explosives for the remote detonation. He had waited for hours at the end of the street for the occupant of the house to leave and give him his opening. Again, though, he was a pro; he had been able to enter through the back door without much trouble, plant the device, and leave without a trace.

After the explosion, he knew what the police would find; something that looked to be a rather crude detonation device – something that someone had built in their own garage, or even bought online. Clearly an intentional effort to lead them to the conclusion that this was a novice job, rather than a professional one.

Now that everything was set, he had only one phone call to make, and he laughed to himself as he looked at the number. It had been scratched onto a small piece of paper, which had been folded into the pocket of his bag. It was typical of his employer, this supreme secrecy; Raul found it tiresome, but he'd learned to deal with it, given the amount of money. He dialed methodically and listened … only two rings.

"Hello?" the voice on the other end answered nervously.

"Boom," Raul answered quietly. He pressed a red button on the remote control device, and his work was done.

Raul hung up the phone, and thought quietly about the poor slob on the other end of the line. He muttered a brief apology for the faceless man. "Shit happens, my friend," he said to himself, pulling the cord from the wall and counting another job done.

He paused for a moment to look out the window; the view was of the downtown lights, which reflected off the rising mist below him. It was a particularly dark night but for the moon, which hung as a small sliver, low in the sky. He turned north and scanned the landscape; there it was. Slight, but very clear, a burst of light with a hint of dark smoke following.

He smiled to himself and placed the small electronic switch back in his suitcase, where he'd already put the phone and the remote control device. He closed and locked the suitcase and headed for the door, leaving behind a few footsteps in the dust, but little else. His associates would be pleased with his progress, and his job was almost done. Only one more task to complete before he could enter his now-official retirement.

Chapter 5

"Damn!" Holly shouted, frustrated. Her team was losing, and she hated it when that happened. The Dallas Stars raced down the ice, crossing the blue line and once again yielding to the other team. The players watched as the puck darted between them.

"Don't you just love hockey?" Holly shouted toward her date, glancing quickly up at him. *Yep, he sure is cute*, she thought to herself. She loved day games too, as it left the rest of the day to do anything else they wanted.

"Yeah, great fights. Stars can't win a game, though," he replied, laughing.

Holly's mouth drew down in a frown as he insulted her team. That certainly wasn't any way to make friends, but at least he was cute. She forced herself to smile back, and reached for the beer she'd been nursing all afternoon. She couldn't afford to get tipsy on the first date. And she'd promised Jeff that she'd call him after the game and let him know that she was okay. He was always too worried about her.

Holly knew that Jeff had taken on a big brother role in her life. And she knew why. She'd been diagnosed with cancer a few years before, and her boyfriend at the time had melted down. This meltdown had materialized as a beating in the very hospital room where she was diagnosed. He had become enraged for reasons that Holly still didn't understand, beating her until her face was black and blue, with tears and blood streaking her cheeks. The nurses and doctor had run in and pulled the man off of Holly before he'd done too much damage, but it had shaken her badly, and made it difficult to trust anyone.

Thankfully, after a surgery and six months of chemo, Holly was now in remission from the cancerous tumor, but the moment she could never forget was when someone she loved tried to take her life.

Jeff was the only person she'd asked the police to call when they arrived at the scene. He was the only one she'd trusted, and the only one she'd wanted to see. Since then, he had taken on the role of protector. She was an only child, and had lost both of her parents many years before in a car crash. In many ways, Jeff and Holly had been thrust together through tragedy. Jeff had lost his wife, and Holly had nearly lost her life. They both found that they were fighters, though, and knew they could lean on each other if they needed to.

The date in question poked her in the ribs now, and motioned toward the stairs. "I'm going to grab another beer. Want something?" He was already halfway out of his seat, heading for the aisle.

"No, thanks," she answered, smiling. When she looked again, he was gone.

She turned back toward the ice, scanning the audience to watch the crowd watch the game, when a face caught her attention. She looked back to try to find what she had seen. Had someone been staring at her? She looked around, but couldn't find whatever it was that had caught her attention. She was probably letting her imagination get the best of her, she thought, trying to focus on the game instead.

After a couple of minutes, though, she turned back to the audience and allowed her eyes to wander again. Almost immediately, she found what had drawn her attention the first time. That face! Brown eyes and small ringlets of long, dark hair. His face was that of a chiseled statue, of Greek origin. Why had he caught her attention?

She glanced down, beginning to feel uncomfortable. He had seen her look back at him, and was staring now. Something was very unusual about his face, though she couldn't decide what it was.

"What's wrong, Holly?" Jack asked suddenly, startling her. She hadn't even realized he had come back, and he was already sitting next to her, with two beers in his hands.

"Brought you a beer, just in case." He looked slyly at her and handed her the beer.

"Just in case, huh?" She smiled back at him.

He nodded. "So what were you looking at up there? You looked spooked."

"Oh nothing, just thought I saw something. Actually ... oh, it's silly. Never mind."

It didn't take much for Jack to forget. He was already cheering the Stars to their next goal. The answer died on Holly's lips, and she glanced at the beer. She didn't look at the strange man again, though she knew that she wouldn't relax again until they'd left the stadium.

Chapter 6

Jeff walked into the front lobby of their office, past the nameplate that read, "Walker, Wright and Turner." The plush carpeting softened his heavy steps and allowed him to enter the office quietly. He was still thinking about Bob's panicked phone call, and the lack of answers this morning. His partner had certainly been spooked last night, and Jeff hoped to get things cleared up with him this morning. But the office was quiet, and Jeff was the first one in. He'd actually had to unlock the door. Very unusual.

The mahogany desk where Jane usually sat had several messages neatly organized in the middle, but nothing else. Jeff grabbed the top messages with his name on them and headed for his corner office, which overlooked the downtown area. He strode quickly across the office and dropped into his leather chair, turning it sideways so he could kick his feet up onto his desk, which had stacks of paper and files strewn across every inch of mahogany. One side of his desk featured the to-be-done files, while the other side held the to-be-done-sooner files. He had quite a sophisticated filing system, if he did say so himself. Jane had been trying to organize him since they opened the doors of the firm, but she'd been unsuccessful.

He knew exactly where everything was. If she organized it, he'd never find anything.

He smiled as he looked over his desk, then glanced quickly at the first of his messages. Another media call. He shook his head; why did they insist on calling? He crumpled the paper and aimed for the trashcan at the other end of the room. The ball of paper hit the rim and bounced into the can. Jeff never missed.

The second message caught his attention. It was from Bob, dated Friday. He didn't remember getting this message on Friday ... he must have missed it. Jeff looked at the clock and realized with a shock that it was almost 11 a.m. He frowned, thinking. Where could Bob be? He always beat Jeff in to work; no matter the occasion, Bob arrived at the office at least an hour before he was scheduled to do so. He was inevitably well prepared, and liked to get to the office early, when it was quiet, to get his best work done. He claimed it helped him think better. He'd always make the coffee first, then grab his first cup and head for his desk to look through his active files.

Not having him here – and not knowing where he was – made Jeff feel edgy and uncomfortable.

He looked at his remaining messages, then set them down and picked up the phone to try Bob again. By the third ring, though, he realized that it was useless. Bob was not near his phone, or was unable to answer. Neither answer was a good one.

Jeff hung up the phone and looked back at his messages for any clues. The third message didn't have a name on it ... and it wasn't Jane's handwriting.

He swallowed, and then read the message aloud. "Bob didn't listen, now maybe you will." He was still staring at the message when the phone rang, making him jump. He answered it on the fourth ring.

"Walker, Wright and Foster, this is Jeff." He waited for a reply, wondering at the silence on the line. "Hello?" he asked again.

"Is this Jeff Walker?" a voice on the other end of the line asked, deep and muffled. The man had some sort of thick accent, but Jeff didn't recognize the voice or the heavily accented English.

"Who's asking?" he asked coolly, stalling.

"A friend," the voice grunted. "You waiting for Bob?" The voice broke into a deep-throated, menacing laugh, and Jeff's mind raced. The accent was Spanish, he thought. Thick, as though the speaker had just recently arrived in the States.

"Who is this, friend?" Jeff asked sharply, sitting up in his leather seat and glancing out the window at the view of downtown.

"That's not important," the voice answered. "What *is* important is that you listen to what I have to tell you. Bob didn't listen, my friend." Jeff listened closely to the accent, using his skills in language to decipher the sound. He could hear that the man had lived in Mexico for many years, but there was something else there.

Cuban, he realized suddenly. The man was Cuban. He continued to listen intently, wondering if this was the same man that had been calling Bob. Until now, Jeff had not received any of these calls.

He was concentrating so deeply that he forgot to blink or take a breath, and realized the lack only when his eyes began to tear.

"Where's Bob, you bastard?" he asked coldly, calculating his next move.

"Listen to me, Jeff. We know that you're working on Project Performance. Stop all of your ties with the White House. Recommend a full reversal of all proposed legislation dealing with Project 42, and I promise that you'll never hear from me again."

"What is this all about? Is this some kind of sick joke?" Jeff struggled to keep his wits about him, while his mind raced back to the project the voice spoke of.

Project Performance was a set of legislative actions designed to hold corporations to higher standards of hiring practices. While it would protect worker's rights, it also pushed forth several very distinct actions to ensure diversity in the workplace. Project 42 was a very specific action within the legislation, and proposed that companies not adhering to a certain percentage of diversity standards be taxed, and taxed heavily. While Jeff knew that this legislation was rather controversial with the old guard politicians and some conservative corporations, he didn't see how that connected back to Bob.

So far, Walker, Wright and Turner was simply consulting with certain members of Congress about drafting the legislation. The efforts were backed, Jeff knew, by large PAC dollars. And everyone knew it was likely to succeed on sheer momentum, dollars invested and cache, since diversity had been the buzzword of the media for the last several years.

He cleared his throat, swallowed again and continued. "I can't stop this project, no matter how much you want me to. Do you know the kind of support it has? It's out of my hands now, and good riddance to it. Even if I did recommend reversal, the House and Senate sub-committees would re-introduce the bills. Forget it. I'm not your man."

The man on the line grunted in displeasure. "Think about it, Jeff. Maybe you should ask Bob what you should do. I think you may change your mind, my friend." With that, there was a click and a dial tone.

Jeff sat, frozen in his seat, still holding the mysterious message in his hand. He shook himself out of his stupor, glanced at the phone, and quickly dialed Bob's number again. He waited for Bob to answer, sitting through five rings. On the sixth ring, the voice mail picked up. Jeff slammed the phone down.

He jumped out of his chair, grabbed his coat and sprinted across the lobby, racing for his car. Bob lived only a mile from the office, and something told him that he needed to see Bob in person. Now. Bob had been receiving these calls for several weeks now, and they had terrified him. Jeff had blown them off, thinking them to be only a prank, but the man on the phone hadn't sounded like he was kidding. Now Jeff counted the days, desperate for hope. When had he last heard from Bob? It had been since Friday, and this was Saturday, and at least three phone calls between then and now, with no answer at Bob's house.

When he got to his car he jumped in and hit the start button, refusing to stop for the signal on his way out of the parking garage.

He flew down the streets, squealed around the corner onto Travis Boulevard, and stomped on the gas. The sight in front of him hit him right between the eyes, though, and he slammed on the breaks. Police cars, fire trucks and a bomb squad car lined the street in front of him. He noticed a column of smoke smoldering at the end of the street.

The smoke was coming from Bob's house, now a charred and smoldering pile of rubble.

Chapter 7

The Stars lost again, but it was such a close game that Holly had hope for the future. Beyond that, the date with Jack was going as well as could be expected.

She glanced back at him now as he grabbed his jacket and joined her in the aisle. They were in a long line of fans, all waiting to exit the arena.

"Jack, it's going to take forever to get out of here!" she sighed, looking around at the mass of people about to converge on the one small exit.

"Leave it to me, Holly," he answered, smiling. He grabbed her hand and proceeded to edge his way down the aisle to an empty row of seats.

"Jack!" she shouted, yanking on his hand. Her legs weren't long enough to step over the seats as easily as he did.

Jack swung one leg over the first row of seats and leaned back to lift her over the seats, with little to no effort, smiling as he did so.

Before she realized what had happened, they were at the exit door. "Nice trick," she laughed, glancing around.

"It was nothing," Jack answered, flashing a sideways grin.

He must have learned that from years of charming women behind the bar, she thought, grinning back.

"Listen, I need to call Jeff. I should probably call him from here." She scanned the hall for a quiet place to make a call. The crowd was loud and the speaker system roared to life with music every time one of the teams scored, fouled or otherwise escalated the game.

"What, he's your keeper?" Jack quipped. He flashed the sideways smile again. "Don't worry, I don't bite."

Holly made a face at him, unappreciative of the joke. "Very funny. I told him I'd call. It won't take very long. Meet me back here in five minutes." She tried to walk away, then realized that he was still holding her hand. "I'll be okay," she insisted, pulling her hand from his.

He nodded. "All right. But be careful, Jeff would kill me if anything happened to you."

Holly nodded, then darted through the crowd to look for a quiet spot to call. When she found a spot around the corner, she pulled her cell phone out and dialed Jeff's number. It was so loud in the building that she could barely hear the phone ringing. She strained to listen, pressing the phone tightly against her ear.

The crowd was shoving and pushing their way through, and Holly had to keep one hand on the column next to the doorway to keep from being drawn back into the surge. She cringed as the phone rang again; *he should be home from the office by now,* she thought. Why wasn't he answering? She looked at her watch and realized it was after 6PM.

That answered that question. He was probably out at a bar somewhere.

After the sixth ring, his voicemail picked up. "Hi, you've reached 690-4536. Leave a message and I'll get back to ya."

She breathed out at the familiar message, and spoke quickly. "Hey, just heading home. It's about 6:30. Give me a call, I should be home around 9 or 10. Since I know you're wondering, Jack's great. I'll fill you in later." She hung up the phone and glanced around to find the best exit. As her eyes passed over the corner near her, she grew still and cautious, though she was careful to keep her eyes moving. Standing away from the crowd was the man she'd seen before.

She froze, watching him out of the corner of her eye, wondering if he'd seen her. He seemed to be waiting for someone. This dark stranger stood out from the crowd, but she'd never seen him before. Why had she noticed him the first time, in a crowd of thousands? She saw him glance her way, and quickly looked down toward the phone again.

She bent over it, sending a quick text message to Jeff as something to do, then hung up the phone and darted toward Jack. This, of course, took her past the stranger, but she'd prepared for that; she kept her head and eyes straight ahead, and glanced at the ground once only, to make sure that he didn't follow her. She had to walk against the crowd to get to Jack, and it took what seemed to be an eternity to find him. He was waiting patiently at the first exit, watching for her, when she got there.

"Did you get him?" he asked nonchalantly.

"No, I'll talk to him later." She looked over her shoulder to find the stranger looking at her again. There was no mistake now – he was definitely looking at her, and he wasn't being shy about it this time. Holly stared right at him, and he didn't look away. She finally broke eye contact and turned back to Jack.

"The strangest thing just happened," she muttered. "Look behind us, at the man with the long hair. He keeps staring at me; do you know who he is?" Holly motioned back toward the corner, where she'd seen the stranger.

"Who?" Jack asked plainly, looking back at where the stranger had been.

Holly looked back and realized that the man had left. "Figures. Never mind, I'm sure it's nothing." She shrugged off the whole incident, anxious to get out of the building.

Jack quickly forgot about her concerns, and moved on with the night. "Where do you want to go now? I can't take you home already – it would ruin my reputation," he joked.

"One drink and then I've got to get home," she answered. Jack nodded, then took her hand and shuffled her out the door, shielding her from the onslaught of the rushing crowd.

"You're talking to the right guy. Drinks are my specialty." He laughed with Holly as they moved swiftly toward the car.

They didn't notice the stranger walking 20 feet behind them, getting out his car keys.

Chapter 8

"I don't give a damn what Congress will support," Lil
yelled into the speaker box. "The people want it, I want it, and
it's going to happen!"

Lil had become passionate about employment law and
had done her thesis on worker's rights in a capital society. This
latest legislation was right up her alley.

There was a long pause, then she spoke again. "You
can't expect me to back down just because some conservative
wonder has stepped up to the podium in the House, wanting to
reverse every piece of goddamn progress we've made in the last
fifteen years. This isn't going to get very far, Phil."

She was having another one of those days. She had one
of the House sub-committee leaders on the phone, explaining
the ill will in Congress over the affirmative action bill, and
things didn't look good.

"Listen, I know how you feel but we can't..." Lil
paused, but didn't let Phil finish what he was saying. "Listen,
Phil, you and I – not to mention the majority of the American
public – believe in equality. I'm not about to let some new kid
on the block send us back to the dark ages."

She paused again to allow him to answer, then snorted.
"Give me a report after the next Congressional session. Oh,
and thanks for your help. Damn it, we just can't let this
continue. Lunch next week? Okay great. Talk to you later."

She punched the "end" button on the phone and sat back, wondering if she'd been too hard on him. She laughed at herself, though, and shook her head. Who was she kidding? Her way with words was legendary, and her direct approach had won over many of the senators and congressmen, not to mention key operatives in the White House. Lil was all business, and she was damn good at what she did. She also attracted attention for her appearance. Her long black hair and defined features were pleasing to most of the male-dominated political system, and she worked hard to stay in shape. She used her appearance to get her where she needed to be, but Lil Turner got what she wanted because she was good at the job as *well* as beautiful.

"Hey George, get in here," she shouted to her assistant. "I need to get a message to the president." She figured she'd go straight to the top with this one.

Her assistant rushed into the room, pen and pad of paper in hand, and waited for the message.

"Set an appointment with him. Let his office know that I need to discuss the women's delegate and the future of the country. We need to talk about what it's coming to, and..." She trailed off, realizing that her assistant had no sense of humor. He was dutifully recording the message, without hearing her sarcasm or acknowledging her ridiculous statements.

"Just set an appointment for myself and Jeff to meet with Bill as soon as possible," she finished, shaking her head.

George made his exit and Lil looked back at her desk, reveling in the moment. It wasn't every day that you had your assistant call the president and expect an answer. She knew she'd get the meeting; her actions over the past several months virtually guaranteed it. Interesting times ... Lil Turner had gained attention in the last several months because the legislation she was consulting on and supporting had big dollars behind it. That kind of momentum and support attracted the interest of the media. Lil had ended up on several talk shows and her charm, wit and knowledge of the issues gained her the spotlight as a political commentator and go-to expert in the matters of employment law, and specifically corporate employment policies. While the topic seemed rather dry, Lil's passion and expertise caused media ratings to actually spike during her media tours. She had become a media – not to mention political – darling.

She shook her head to get rid of the daydreams and reached for a pen and paper. She needed to write up an addendum to the initiative her office had been working on so diligently; it was the same initiative that was getting them so much attention, and it was her job to make sure that it continued to do so.

Project Performance was becoming a thorn on the side for most Republicans and conservative Democrats. Congress didn't know what to do with it. A majority of the American public, as well most of Congress, had supported the bill until the recent change of face. Now this mysterious group, which called themselves World One, appeared to be threatening the successful passing of the bill. She didn't understand it, but this group had somehow reached some very influential people on the hill.

This meant that there were some people that didn't like the bill she'd been supporting and consulting on, and they were getting stronger in the newly conservative atmosphere. She'd heard several very direct threats against the bill and those who supported it. If pressed, she would have admitted that she could see why.

The bill took the diversity movement one step further by enacting several steep tax implications for corporations not adhering to the minimum percentage diversity requirements. The bill specifically required that 20 percent of executive-level positions be filled with women and/or those of a protected diversity class, and that 35 percent of the workforce be of a protected diversity class. Many conservatives saw this as hamstringing corporations. It was a tough issue, but most agreed that the current rates of diversity employment were pretty dismal. The agreement on the methodology for improving those statistics was where things got a bit dicey. When it came to big politics and big money, things got ugly, and fast.

Lil knew that she had her work cut out for her. There were some strong political forces at the top, and they were trying to derail all of her efforts toward equalizing the work force and opportunities. This was an important bill – it would change things, and it could save people. By changing the face of the workforce, and extending opportunities to those that never got that chance, the bill would create a stronger America. Bringing money and influence to neighborhoods that had been neglected and forgotten would strengthen America's resolve to be better. She knew it. And she wasn't about to go down without a fight.

She sat back in her plush leather chair and looked out the tall window behind her desk, trying to pull her mind back around to her work. She needed a reset, she knew, and she loved to catch up on the news. Reaching out, she grabbed the remote and turned on the small TV in her office.

"...It occurred around 9:30 p.m. Friday night. The victim had allegedly been receiving threatening phone calls from an unknown source. Sources indicate that this bombing was tied somehow to Project Performance. The White House issued a statement that it will begin a full investigation into the matter..."

Lil sat up abruptly, her eyes flying to the TV. Hearing the words 'Project Performance' had caught her attention, and she leaned in. The image on the TV showed a street lined with police cars. She looked closely and recognized the street name.

Her heart raced, and she caught her breath. Why was she seeing Bob's street on the news? Why were there police cars there? Come to think of it – if there were news crews on the street, why hadn't she heard from Bob? Was he in trouble?

As she continued to watch, she received her answers. There, at the end of the street, where Bob's sprawling suburban house once sat, was a smoldering pile of debris. The reporter stood in front of the yellow crime scene tape to the left of the screen, leaving the right side to display the horror. The front door frame and a few bricks clinging to each side was all that could be discerned of what once was a house. But there it was, just to the right of the doorframe, clinging to the bricks – the metal wreath Lil had given him last Christmas. He'd left it up all year long. And now it seemed to be the only thing that survived.

Just outside the rubble were scorched trees; and beyond that were horrified bystanders looking on at the perimeter of the yellow tape. She threw her head into her hands, struggling to breathe. As hard as she tried, though, she couldn't process all that she was seeing. What had happened? Was Bob dead? Had he been home when that happened? Who could have done this? The questions raced through her mind, threatening to drive her mad, until she turned in her seat and yelled out the door to her assistant.

"George, get in here! Have you heard about this? Why hasn't anyone informed me of this?"

George rushed in to find Lil leaning close to the small TV on the credenza in her office. She'd turned the volume up as loud as it would go, and was hanging on the words of the reporter.

"Bob Wright was a political consultant with the well-known firm Walker, Wright and Turner, which focuses on special interest programs and has strong ties to the White House. Mr. Wright, along with his partners Jeff Walker and Lil Turner, were spearheading some legislation that furthered the affirmative action agenda. The Project Performance..."

"Jeff, have you heard the news?" Lil was already dialing Jeff at the office in Dallas. She had started working out of their Washington, D.C. satellite office as soon as the new Congress was introduced, and hadn't seen her partners in months.

She was put through to Jeff's voicemail, but continued her message, assuming that he was busy with other problems. "What happened to Bob? Unbelievable! Did the phone calls have anything to do with this? Call me back as soon as you can. And watch your back down there."

She hung up the phone, knowing that she had sounded as panicked as she felt, and turned to her assistant. "George, forget calling the president's office. I'll call him myself. This is a crisis situation."

She looked down at her desk and her thoughts drifted to Bob Wright. He'd been a long-time college friend and business partner, and hadn't wanted to handle this particular piece of legislation. She'd insisted, though, telling him how important it was, and he'd given in. If the bombing was actually about Project Performance, then it was her fault that he'd been killed.

"And call someone down at the DPD. Who do we know down there? Was it Foster?" Lil thought for a minute, and snapped her fingers to emphasize her thought. "Foster Grant. Give him a call and find out what the hell happened. See if they have any leads on who bombed Bob's house." This thought hit her squarely in the gut as the reality set in.

George told her that he'd get right on it and left the room. She watched him go, and then placed her hands over her face in amazement and shock. *What has this come to?* she wondered. She knew of the calls that Bob had been getting. She also knew that Bob had uncovered something – something potentially very explosive. She realized now that perhaps they should have taken the threatening calls more seriously, and wondered if all of their lives were in danger. She needed to find what Bob had found, and quick, so that she knew what they were dealing with.

"And George..." This time she hit the intercom button to his desk and spoke softly. "Book me on the next flight to Dallas."

Chapter 9

"I'm sorry, sir, I can't let you in here. This area is closed for investigation." The officer looked firmly at Jeff, holding one hand against his chest.

Jeff grunted in frustration. This was the third time he'd been through this, and he was starting to lose his patience. "Listen, I knew Bob. Christ, he was my business partner. I know all about the phone calls and the..."

His voice broke as he tried to control himself, and he looked to the end of the street, where Bob's house was still smoldering – practically leveled – and coughed. Large pieces of debris were scattered in the street, and he could see Bob's car, crushed in the driveway. *Where's my partner in all of that?* he wondered. Had the man been killed immediately, or had he been injured, and died a slow and painful death?

I should have believed him, he thought bitterly. *I should have been there for him.*

"Let me talk to the officer in charge, at least," Jeff argued. "I need to find out what happened."

"Pull to the side and let me talk to my lieutenant." The young officer, a man in his twenties, walked over to the middle of the scurry of investigators, officers and firemen, who were all trying to secure the area for the inevitable investigation.

Five minutes later, another officer walked over to Jeff and asked him to join them at the end of the street. Jeff jumped out of his car to join the rest of the crowd, scanning the faces for friends.

"Mike tells me you knew the victim," one of the officers said dryly. "What was your relationship to Bob Wright?"

"He is – was – my business partner. What the hell happened here?" Jeff breathed deeply, trying to control his body's shaking.

The officers ignored his question, asking him another instead. "Did you talk to him last night?"

"No, he left a message on my recorder around 9. He was in a panic again over another prank phone call. He started getting them about a month ago. I told him it was nothing. Do you think it's related?"

"We checked his phone records, and he received a phone call originating from an empty hotel room around 9:30 last night. The explosion occurred around the same time. We don't know yet if they're related."

Another officer held up his hand and turned toward Jeff. "I need to ask you a few more questions," he muttered. "Where were you last night?"

"You've got to be kidding!" Jeff sputtered, enraged. "What do you mean, where was I last night? What exactly are you implying? You're crazy! He is my damn business partner!"

"Listen, sir, this is routine questioning. I understand how you feel. But I must ask you where you were last night."

Jeff shook his head, shocked. "I was playing cards with a friend of mine. Call Holly Darling and ask her where I was."

The whole scene was becoming a blur. It was unreal. Bob couldn't be dead, and they couldn't actually be asking him where *he'd* been during the explosion. What on earth had happened? Did it have anything to do with the prank calls? What about that message he'd had this morning, and the call after it?

Suddenly his heart dropped. The caller had said that Bob would learn his lesson. He'd threatened the same for Jeff. Jeff ground his teeth together, the anger building in his head. *That bastard isn't going to scare me*, he thought, his mind racing. The man had killed Bob, and now he was threatening Jeff. The next step was obvious: Jeff was going to have to find the bastard who did this and put an end to it.

He glanced over to the police blockade halfway down the street, and noticed a familiar face. He was shocked; it was Victoria. A police officer was talking to her and helping her into a car. She started to drive away, and Jeff found himself running after her. By the time he got there, though, she was gone. He turned to the officer who had helped her to her car.

"What was that woman doing here?" he asked, huffing with the run.

"Who are you and what are *you* doing here?" the officer returned, frowning.

"I was a friend of his." Jeff motioned angrily toward the destroyed house and raised his voice to get the officer's attention.

Why had Victoria been there? How was she involved? Did she know Bob? His mind raced with questions, and only one answer: He needed to get to the bottom of this, and he knew just who to call to help him.

Chapter 10

"Listen, Raul took care of it. I don't want to hear it. That bill can't pass, do you understand me? We need to stop it, by any means necessary. And I mean *any* means necessary. If he starts causing problems, then eliminate him. And don't worry about her. She's a woman. We'll scare the hell out of her with what we do to her partners. In fact, she's probably packing her bags right now."

Al was tired of his nervous associates, and found himself wishing – for the millionth time – that they had his experience and nerve. He was going to see this thing through; he had a lot riding on this next move, and he wasn't about to throw it all away. The influence of his organization was going to grow, and this was just the first step in guaranteeing that future. Washington would soon see that he was a dominant force, and a power to be reckoned with. They would see that he was running their government for them – making the decisions he wanted made, and killing the movements he didn't like. They would have to stop turning away from him, soon. His organization's plan was beginning to fall into place, now, and that meant that his time was coming.

Stan Flemming – the man on the other end of the line – had been a great front man. He was squeaky clean, good looking, and the perfect face guy for the organization. He had done a good job, and he'd kept the attention on himself rather than the organization behind him. Al had to remind himself of this as he listened to Stan, who was now starting to get restless. The man didn't have the stomach to deal with the necessary death and destruction, and now he was trying to pull out. Al had known it was a possibility, but he needed the man to hold on for just a little while longer. He put on his most convincing voice and continued.

"Right now, Raul is waiting for my phone call. I told him to lay low in D.C. and await my orders. He should fit in with all the other loons out there – no one will notice him. If I need him to move, I'll let him know." Al thought of how his actions had sent shockwaves of fear through Washington. That mighty government was shaken. The thought pleased him and put a smile across his face, though he knew that this was just the first step.

"Thanks Stan, you've done a fantastic job. We are very proud and we are close. I'll be in touch," he finished, hanging up the phone.

They were getting so close. They had Washington chasing their tails around a piece of legislation that, quite frankly, he didn't care about. They'd been working that angle, though, and using it as the stress point for their next move. It had been fun to watch everyone running around with their tails tucked between their legs, in response to the threats sent through his veiled associates. This distraction was exactly what he needed, and all part of a great plan that had been put into action many decades before. His father would be proud of how far he'd come, and how close he was to reaching the goal.

"How easy it is to shake up this town," Al laughed. He threw his head back in glee as he paced through his living room, then turned toward his associate, who sat on the couch.

"You're fuckin' crazy," Gordon noted, watching his boss pace across the floor. He was there to wait for his next order, and had been there to witness firsthand Al's reaction to the bombing news. It had been chilling.

"Crazy, huh? It's a game, my friend, and it's too easy. I'm telling you, we need them to keep fighting about those bills, keep getting scared about the threats. We need to keep them wondering who's going after them. That's how we keep them looking the other way. I want no mistakes. If you see any hesitation, call them at home, call them at their office. No mistakes."

He stopped directly in front of Gordon and stared into his eyes. "None." His breath was stale, and Gordon drew back from it. "And get me a list of how many we have recruited into our organization. I want a full report. Soon we will not be ignored. Washington will be surprised to find out who's on our side. Having them run around this bill will keep them busy for a while. By the end of it, we'll be in the driver's seat and they'll never know what hit them." He laughed mightily again at the thought, full of his own power.

"Yes boss."

"They should be scared shitless now, and I shouldn't have any problem getting them to cooperate," his boss continued.

Gordon nodded quietly, standing his ground until the other man had finished. He never backed down from this man or any other; that was why Al kept him around.

Al's face finally relaxed and he turned, throwing one arm around his employee. "I know you'll take care of it, friend." He paused, thinking. "You're still trailing the girl?"

"Yeah, nothing to report there. Stefano is on her. He'll let me know if we need to take action. Nothing to report yet. Went to a hockey game with some bartender from Brooklyn, but she hasn't been with Jeff since Friday. We got into her house and tapped her phone while they were at the game. Looks like she's still out with him now, at a bar. We have her covered. Should be a piece of cake." Gordon smiled at his boss, confident of his men and information.

"Good work. We'll reel them in soon."

Chapter 11

Stefano sat quietly in his car, huddled deep inside his fleece coat. He sipped his steaming coffee and glanced occasionally across the street to the Fog City Diner. A couple wandered in or out every few minutes; the place was hopping tonight. He hadn't seen the couple he was watching for yet, but that didn't mean that he wouldn't.

He watched intently as another couple exited the diner, but it wasn't who he was looking for. It could be hours before he saw them again, so he settled in for the long haul. He couldn't go into the diner to find her or keep an eye on her; he'd already taken too many chances tonight, and there would be hell to pay if anyone found out. For now, he had to be patient – they couldn't leave without passing him, and when they did, he'd be ready.

***

Inside the diner, Holly was having a terrific time, her mind far from the strange man at the hockey game.

"This is a great place, Jack!" she said as they walked toward a seat by a window in the back.

"It's always packed here. Opened up not too long ago," Jack shouted back. They both turned and twisted, maneuvering their way through the crowded restaurant to the reasonably quiet table in the far corner.

As they sat down, Jack motioned to the waiter. "Sir, we'll start off with a couple of beers." He winked at Holly as the waiter smiled in answer.

"What's the occasion?" Holly joked. "Beer must be to you like champagne is to normal people."

"Listen, I may not be as polished as some of your other friends, but I'm not a fake either. I see all kinds from behind that bar. And I usually don't like what I see." He was giving Holly that now-famous grin.

"I didn't mean anything by that. I just meant..." Holly paused. She hadn't meant to offend him, but getting out of it was going to be tricky. "I meant that I like your style. Really, I feel comfortable around you, and I barely know anything about you. It's funny, to be honest." She grew quiet, thinking about what she'd said and the truth of the statement. Her mind wandered for a moment to that strange face at the game, which tugged at her distrust and brought up some very familiar fear. Then she turned back to the diner and her date.

"Not funny at all. It's all happening for a reason, Holly." Jack savored saying her name, drawing it out into a sexy drawl, and they both grew silent and awkward.

Holly looked at the man in front of her and gave herself a mental shake. *I don't know what I'm doing*, she thought suddenly. *I must be crazy.*

She knew that she had a soft spot for "bad boys," and wondered if she was falling back into her old habits. But Jack seemed nice, he really did. It was so good to be out with a man, flirting, and Jack was certainly attractive. In fact, she found that she really liked him. Perhaps seeing the stranger's face again and again, and not being able to reach Jeff, just had her a bit anxious.

After her last relationship had ended with a police report, she'd found herself reluctant to get close to any man that wasn't Jeff. He had been her protector, as well as her best friend. She was definitely having fun with Jack, but that tugging notion that she wasn't safe had crept into her thoughts and she couldn't shake it. She was reaching out to Jeff to get that familiar, safe voice, and since she couldn't reach him, she knew the best thing was to tell Jack how much fun she had but that she was tired and it was time to go home. Years of counseling had taught her that she would fight that feeling of being safe, and that it was her job to make sure when those feelings crept up that she dealt with them. She cursed herself for letting her old fears creep in on her night of fun; she just wanted to have fun again without the past pulling her back down.

If she could just talk to Jeff, he would calm her fears and she wouldn't have to end the evening.

Suddenly the waiter appeared next to the table, leaning over to place the two beers in front of them. "Ah, the drinks,"

Holly muttered, relieved to be saved from the awkward moment with Jack.

She glanced at her beer, then up at Jack, and made a decision. "Listen, I'm going to try Jeff one more time. He's got to be home by now. I'll be right back." She didn't wait for a response from Jack, but grabbed her purse and darted toward the back of the restaurant.

She didn't really *need* to call Jeff, she realized, but was also looking for a good excuse to leave the table. Jack was cute, but she wasn't positive that he was her type, and the sudden intensity, and sense that Jack may want more, had made her uncomfortable. This was nothing new, though it was something she'd only noticed in the last year; she was fine with flirtation and fun, but when a man seemed to want more from her, she found herself drifting quickly away, mentally. Calling Jeff again was the perfect excuse for drifting in the physical sense as well.

She reached the back of the restaurant and pulled her cell phone out to dial his number. After a couple of rings, she got his voicemail again.

"Jeff, Holly here," she growled, frustrated. Where on earth *was* the man? "You're probably thinking I'm not havin' a good time. Why would I be calling you? Nah, havin' a great time. Yep." She paused for dramatic effect, allowing herself a long, deep breath. "Well, uh, I'll see you tomorrow, I suppose. And I want to talk to you about this weird guy I saw at the game. Strange thing, and it kind of creeped me out. Well, I'll talk to you later."

She hung up the phone, wondering where Jeff was and whether he was safe. As she turned back toward the table, her eyes ran to the window at the corner. Something there caught her eye.

***

Stefano looked at his watch. They'd been in there for over an hour. *Must be a good date*, he thought to himself. But he didn't have this kind of time to waste. He looked back to the restaurant and tried to make out the faces through the front windows. That beautiful redhead, where was she? It was too bad that he had to find her this way, he thought. He rather liked her ... but it wasn't possible.

"It's 5, where is she?" he asked himself, scanning the windows again. That steroid stud with her wasn't her type, and it shouldn't have taken this long for him to take her home. Stefano prided himself in knowing women. And he wanted to know this one.

He looked up at the windows again, and happened to look through to her standing by the phone. She caught his gaze and stared right back.

"Damn," he muttered, ducking. She was smart – he liked that – but now he wondered. She had seen something ...

had it been him? He could have sworn that she was looking right at him, but that might be paranoia on his part. Those green eyes were piercing, and his imagination was getting the best of him again. No way she'd actually been looking at him; she'd never seen him before, that he knew of. True, she'd looked at him at the hockey game, but there had been thousands of people there. He had been careful to park his car across the street under a dark tree anyhow, and his face should be in complete darkness. That had been the plan, anyway.

He glanced cautiously back, and saw that she had continued quickly toward the table and sat with her back to the window. She didn't look back, so his guess was that she hadn't seen anything. Stefano was not as cautious at the game as he should have been, and he knew it, but he was intrigued by her. He'd wanted to see her more closely.

This assignment was going be tough, he thought, watching her full auburn hair swing against her back. Still, the job right now was simple: Stay as close as possible to her, and record her every move. It gave him a chance to keep staring at her, at least.

***

Holly sat down and grabbed the frosty beer in front of her, chugging half of it down with one gulp.

Jack stared at her in amazement. "Very impressive. Where'd you learn to do that?"

"Years of having guy friends, Jack. Just one of the many useful things they've taught me," she said with a wink and laugh. She ran her tongue over her lips, enjoying the smooth feel of the cold beer.

She took another drink, finishing her beer in three gulps, and then looked at Jack's still half-full beer. At that moment, she felt her sixth sense creeping in again. Jeff had actually taught her quite a bit about being alert, and her mind was finally catching up with the implications of having seen the same stranger's face multiple times in one night. It wasn't a coincidence. It simply wasn't. She had been writing it off, but now the tingling on the back of her neck was getting worse, and she realized that something wasn't right.

Those phone calls that Jeff's partner had been getting ... Jeff's silence ... the stranger at the hockey game, and now outside ... she needed to get home. Was there a connection? Jeff and Holly's friendship was no secret. Were the threats to Jeff's office leading to someone now looking for her? That would mean that she was in danger, and that she needed to get someplace safe. Yes, it was time to end the night. Besides, it was getting late...

Jack read her nervous fidgeting and decided that now would be the best time to end the evening. "Holly, listen, if you want to go home that's no problem. I'll take you," he said quietly.

She smiled. "Oh, Jack, I hope you know it's not you. This has been great. I just have so many things to do and it's getting late."

Jack didn't even wait for her to finish. "Holly, your wish is my command." He laughed at his own joke, trying to ease the tension, and she smiled back.

Jack paid the tab and pulled the chair out for her, surprising her. As they walked out of the restaurant, they both stopped to take a deep breath of the fresh, cool evening air. She loved the cool evening air blowing through her hair. He guided her down the stairs, and she looked up when they reached the last step. Her eyes focused on a man across the street.

"That's him!" she muttered under her breath. She turned and tugged Jack quickly toward the car.

He pulled back, confused. "Hey, what's going on?"

She motioned to the man across the street with her eyes. "The guy from the game. Remember, the one I tried to point out to you, the guy who'd been bothering me? That's him across the street. Why is he following me?" She wasn't trying to hide the sheer fear in her voice, and feeling her body begin to shiver, reached up to pull her coat more tightly around her.

Jack put his arm around her and led her quickly to the car, glancing at the black Mustang parked across the street.

"Holly, get in the car. I'll take care of this asshole."
He didn't wait for Holly to respond, but locked her in the car
and started quickly toward the Mustang.

Whoever the stranger was, he didn't wait to chat with
Jack. He'd already started the car and squealed into gear by the
time Jack was in the road. Now he gunned the car, aiming
straight for Jack.

Chapter 12

"God, Lil, I knew something was wrong. Damn it, if I had just called Bob when I said I would, none of this damn mess would've happened." Jeff paced back and forth in their office as Lil sat quietly in the leather chair adjacent to his mahogany desk.

"Jeff," Lil said abruptly, "there's no reason for this to have happened. But it did, and it doesn't have a damn thing to do with me, you, or anybody else. Some assholes out there wanted him dead. Hell, maybe it was just a random prank, like you thought, and it went too far. But we've got to find out who did this and why."

She was putting on her best show, but underneath the tough exterior she was hurt and scared. She really loved Bob. This threatened her tough resolve and she was trying hard to focus.

Bob was the only person she'd turned to; he enabled her to be strong and fearless. What would she be without him? She still struggled with the concept of him being gone. After a long day, he was the one who held her for hours, telling her everything was going to be ok. He was the only one who saw her softer side. Who would see it now? She shook her head; who would listen to her, who was left that knew who she really was? Everyone knew Bob was the person you could count on. So what now?

The last time she'd seen him, he had flown to Washington to meet her at one of the political luncheons. They'd done the appropriate amount of networking with everyone, and then left quietly to find a nice restaurant, where they could catch up over a glass of wine.

Lil had loved Bob since the first time they'd met in college. And Bob had always felt the same. They'd kept their romance quiet, as they didn't want it to distract from their work, but there was no mistake – they were very much in love, and they both knew it. They'd had plans to go to Cabo together in a month. Bob had been teasing her for months about that trip, telling her that it was bigger than she realized, and that it might change their lives. Later, she would find an engagement ring amongst his things; a sign that he'd finally meant to take their relationship to the next level.

Now her mind raced. She lowered her face into her hands once again, and let go of the reins she'd been holding so tightly. This time, she sobbed. Finally she looked up at Jeff.

"Does this have anything to do with the threats Bob had been getting and the harassing calls about the bill?" she asked, voicing her thoughts out loud. "Who would be interested in whether this bill is passed or defeated? It doesn't make any sense. I know it's a controversial topic, and it's on everyone's mind on Capitol Hill, but why kill for it?"

Her thoughts wandered again to Bob, and she worked to choke back her emotions. This problem called for rational thought, not the emotions of a hurt friend and lover.

"It doesn't make any sense, Lil, no sense at all," Jeff agreed. He stopped his pacing long enough to look at her, and realized suddenly that she was having a tough time with all of this. He was the only one who knew what had been going on between Lil and Bob. She had to act tough now, but he knew that this must be tough as hell for her.

He reached over to grab her hand and grasped it tightly. "We'll find these bastards, Lil, I promise. We'll find them." He knew that he was talking to both himself and Lil as he said it, trying to give them both some comfort. He also knew that it was too little. It wouldn't bring Bob back, and it would never fill the hole that he'd left in their lives. Sighing, he turned to look out onto the downtown Dallas skyline. The sun was a distant thought on the horizon, barely visible beyond the towering, glittering buildings. It was another clear night, just like the night on which Bob had died. His thoughts raced through everything that had happened over the last week. Nothing made sense, but he knew that the answer must be there, somewhere. There must be something, some sort of clue about who they were dealing with. Maybe he knew the killer, or the man controlling the killer. There must be some link...

He thought of his friends in the intelligence community, searching for someone who could help. They would know more than he would, and maybe give him some sort of direction. He pulled out his phone and dialed a familiar number, hoping that he was right, and that it would help him get to the bottom of this.

Chapter 13

Victoria watched the lawn below as a man walked slowly up to the side of the building to a fire escape. In what seemed like only a moment she watched Stefano step through the window she had left open.

"They must never suspect, do you understand?" She pronounced every word strongly and carefully, as though she was talking to a child. Al was counting on her to carry this through, and he wasn't someone you disappointed. She remained cool on the outside, but her own doubts were finding their way to the surface. Her interest and connection with him could prove fatal, she knew. She must remain focused on the task at hand.

Jeff must remain expendable, and her feelings or interest in him must never give her hand away. She had known Jeff since his days in the National Security Agency (NSA), when she had worked there as well and was assigned to watch him. He'd never known about it. She'd tracked his every move, though, and had gotten to know him, and appreciated his prowess in getting the information he needed. He had almost been too good, and his bosses had asked her to keep an eye on him, for fear that he was getting too close to the enemy.

Back then, Victoria's job was simple – to watch and report.

She never found anything on him, though, and she was ultimately re-assigned, but his story lingered on with her. She'd grown attached to him as she watched him, and had even developed a bit of a crush. She was always sorry to leave him behind, and wondered what they would have become if they could have met.

That had been a long time ago, and the road that had led from trailing Jeff to working for Al ... well. She sighed, pulling her mind back to the present. And to have him find her now seemed like a very big coincidence. She knew that she could never show or act on her latent feelings for him. She knew that she couldn't admit to having seen him before. Neither Al nor Stefano knew anything of her past, and she wanted to keep it that way. They knew nothing about her, and yet they thought they did.

Stefano's voice pulled her back to the conversation. "Of course, never. You know who you're dealing with? I'm a professional, and I've never had any trouble. Raul is the best, and so am I."

He watched her carefully, admiring her well-kept body. Her hair caught the light from the street.

"Listen, if he gets close, you must disappear. We've had too many close calls. It was convenient that he followed me, but I can't have any mistakes." She flipped her hair as she walked toward the window. "I have a lot riding on this." A sly smile crossed her face, turning her lips up.

Al had paid her a lot of money to keep an eye on Jeff and his law firm, and Jeff finding his way into her club had been a fortuitous occurrence. Her boss didn't care if a flirtation turned to more, as long as it led Jeff down the wrong path, and kept him off Al's tail. She knew that she was using the opportunity to explore the possibilities of a relationship with Jeff. It wouldn't be so hard – she'd just have to keep him thinking that she was a singer at the club, and protect him from trouble. Maybe someday she would tell him the truth, but maybe not.

Victoria knew she was dangerously close to the edge, and entangled in this double life. At times she yearned for a simple life, one where truth was constant and where her life wasn't always on the line. And yet she knew there was something in her blood that kept her coming back for the danger. She lived and breathed adrenalin and, for now, she knew no other life. She'd been doing it for so long that she didn't know what she'd do without it.

Looking up at Stefano again, she smiled, thinking that she was right where she needed to be.

Chapter 14

Months Earlier, Conference Room, Washington, D.C. Hilton

The conference room was filled to capacity. Lil scanned her audience closely, and found that most of them were familiar faces. Bob had invited a few more representatives – people who she had not yet met. She made a mental note to have him introduce them after her presentation, then walked confidently to the front of the room, smiling at the new faces.

"Welcome, everyone. Of course, you all know why you're here. Let's hope I have something enlightening to share, to make it worth your while." She smiled again, knowing that she did indeed have important information to share, and her audience snickered at her humor. Getting anything more than a snicker from any group in Washington was nothing short of a miracle, so she considered this a great accomplishment.

"This is a very distinguished group," she continued. "Each of you has a big job and big expectations from your constituencies. I hope to show you today why affirmative action interests are more important now than they were when they were first inaugurated into our democratic nation. They benefit society as a whole. I will show you how these bills have positively affected our society today ... how each of us has benefited from the effects of these interests."

She watched her audience closely for any doubts or interest and paused, allowing them to digest what she had said. The intensity in the room grew. Everyone was waiting on her next words, waiting to hear why she'd called them to meet today.

"To date, across the country, approximately 500,000 individuals have been employed as a result of these affirmative action bills. Those are 500,000 individuals who would not have received this employment without the right legislation," she continued swiftly.

"Reverse discrimination has been the primary objection to these bills. And today these issues are already being addressed..." Lil understood that most of her audience agreed with her logic, but she also knew that most of the audience members were white males. As such, they didn't necessarily want to see reverse discrimination, but they also didn't feel that they had any direct benefit from affirmative action. Her job was to bring it home for them, make them see that they *did* in fact benefit from the legislation. She stepped closer to the gentlemen at the front of the room. They were seated at an oblong table, which was shined and waxed so efficiently that the reflections of the light almost blinded her. The gentlemen's brows lowered in concentration as they listened to her words.

"Discrimination is wrong, no matter what the discrimination might be. In America, we all have something to contribute. It is each person's responsibility to find the individual who contributes best to each job, and hire without discrimination based on race, creed, color or nationality. That is the very heart and soul of the American constitution. And beyond that, we are supporting those who cannot get jobs. How about social security for the unemployed or single mothers ... how can we continue to support them when we can't even balance the budget? We're spending money on them that we simply don't have to spend. Let's enable each of these capable individuals to support themselves instead. Let's enact tougher laws around discrimination. Let's develop a system that supports better access to education. Let's have strong job training and a six-month mandatory employment time, during which they must be taken off unemployment and welfare. This is all part of Project Performance. You see, there's more to this idea than meets the eye."

She paused to grab a quick sip of water from her glass. Everyone in the room was watching, waiting for her next statement. She carefully replaced the glass in its former position at the head of the table and continued, looking long and hard at her audience.

"You and I both are lucky. We're here because someone somewhere gave us a shot. Someone gave us a chance to prove ourselves. But imagine yourself in a position where no one is willing to give you that chance, and the only reason they won't is because of the color of your skin, or where you live. We're also addressing reverse discrimination with this bill. Quotas are not our focus; we just want the right person for the right job. And within our effort lies equality in education.

"Give people the same access to education, and we will all rise to our best abilities." She focused on her audience. Everyone's gaze was glued to her, and she knew she had their attention. Now was the time to let the other shoe drop.

This particular piece of legislation was drawing a lot of attention, and some of it was negative. There were firms and powerful individuals who stood against the bill, and were going out of their way to fight it. Lil knew that World One, an organization run by businessman Stan Flemming, was somehow at the center of the opposition to the progress of Project Performance. Her partner Bob had discovered more about World One, and it had solidified that assumption. For Project Performance to move forward, she had to defeat organizations like World One. And it started here, and now. She wanted to put this organization on notice publicly, by calling out their antics in front of the rest of the businessmen in the room.

"World One must not be acknowledged. Their intention is to intimidate and force a vote against these bills. They campaign as though they're fighting for all Americans, but you don't have to look too closely to see that they are fighting for one cause and one cause only. They want to control our actions, to the detriment of all facets of our government. They want to tell us what to think, and, worse, what to do. Look more closely, and you'll see that their membership is veiled – there is no published list. And any attempt to get such a list is futile. Believe me, I've tried. Why would their members want to be disguised if they have such a legitimate cause? Why must they hide if they're an honest, above-board company? If you want to stop them, if you want to keep our government intact and in control, then make sure we're the ones making decisions. Not them."

Lil knew that the membership list of World One was cloaked and protected, and decided that now was the time to call that into question.

"Ask Stan Flemming who the members of World One are. Ask him why they've kept themselves secret. Does he even know, himself? Let's find out.

"The point is," she continued, her voice firm, "you must act now. Act smartly. Act swiftly. Just act, before it's too late." Her voice faded away after her conclusion, and the entire room stood in unexpected and enthusiastic applause.

She smiled, pleased at her success. "Thank you. I hope to see all of your signatures on Project Performance." Lil walked up to Bob, who stood at the back, and he took her around the room, introducing her to the people she didn't know. She watched him out of the corner of her eye as they networked; Bob was really quite impressive in his stature, confidence, and swift and poignant conversation. He also seemed to have a finger on the pulse of all the important Senate and House representatives. Lil knew he was a great asset to the firm.

"And of course you know the Speaker of the House, Lil." Lil extended a firm hand to Speaker Sullivan and smiled at him.

"Very impressive, Ms. Turner. I had heard you were quite good with words. Let's see if you can back that up." Mr. Sullivan did not try to hide his open challenge.

Their eyes met, and neither looked away, though Lil raised one eyebrow in acceptance of the challenge.

Finally Bob insisted that Lil continue on, to meet another new senator from Tennessee. He laughed as they walked away, telling her to be careful about picking fights. They concluded their tour at the back of the room, and fell into their seats as the last of the audience filed out.

"Bob, keep your ears and eyes open on this World One. I don't know where they came from, but I've already heard several government officials asking questions about them. They seem to be getting to the right people. We must stop their voice before it becomes confusing to the rest of the world. Our voting public already has enough messages attacking them from the media. One more group like this will send them over the edge on this issue. It's no wonder we've been apathetic for so long – it's impossible for us to process all of these messages, so we just tune them all out. Who knows what's true and what isn't anymore." She looked squarely at Bob.

He smiled at Lil, who never stopped. "Okay, okay. And by the way, good job. I think you got their attention. Let's just hope it worked." They both stood to make their grand exit to their next appointment with the big guy.

"Let's go see the president." Bob looked at Lil and winked.

"I thought you'd never ask," she laughed. She leaned in toward him as his eyes grew soft, and reveled in how much he loved her. They were truly very lucky, she thought, to be working together on such an important piece. He took her arm and they walked out the door and down the hall. By the time they were near her car, they were holding hands. They had worked hard to keep their love affair a secret, now it seemed they no longer cared.

Bob opened the door for Lil and she slipped into the Audi, while he walked around to the driver's door and jumped in. The minute he was sitting, he leaned over to kiss her. "Great job today," she heard him say.

"Thanks, Bob."

"We are up against some big guns. It's going to be tough and perhaps even dangerous, but we'll fight it together."

"Yes we will."

Chapter 15

Jeff stared into his drink and cleared his mind for a moment. The crowd seemed distant, though he was right in the middle of it. His thoughts began to race back through the past couple of days, and he closed his eyes tightly, as if this would stop them. It didn't, as he'd known it wouldn't, and he allowed his thoughts to drift as they would. He'd have to deal with it at some point, anyhow.

Bob's house had been absolutely decimated; there'd been virtually nothing left. The worst part was that Bob had been trying to reach him the very night it had happened, and he'd been unavailable. He was angry with himself for not being more alert. He should have seen this coming, should have suspected that something was wrong, but he was off his game. He should have paid attention that those calls weren't pranks, even if he didn't know exactly what they were. Bob sure had, and he'd tried to tell him.

Now he was gone, leaving a whole lot of questions. Who was behind this? What had it meant? What did they want? How was Victoria involved? Why was she at Bob's house, talking to the police there? Was this all connected?

He opened his eyes slowly and looked up at the bartender. All he had to do was tip his glass for the man to fix him another 7 & 7. Before Jeff knew it, he had two glasses in front of him.

He gulped down the last of his drink and realized he had lost count. Was this five or six? God, he thought, why Bob? His thoughts drifted back to his last conversation with him.

Jeff made a call to his friend in the NSA, who was also with a small military intelligence group. He called this particular contact only rarely, as it was a name he needed to be cautious with. The man was almost always under very heavy cover, and couldn't always take outside calls safely. However, now definitely seemed the time, and Jeff had need of both information and guidance. His friend went by the name of

Kevin, and even Jeff didn't know his real name or identity. This man had been under cover for many years, his story re-written again and again until his real life was long gone.

Jeff had tried the central number used for operatives. Given his background, he had a standing status as, on occasion, he continued to provide intelligence on a range of national security issues. This time, however, he was simply in need of information himself. He had to provide the litany of secure passwords and reference points to follow the normal security protocol, but even then he was put on hold, where he was kept for over twenty minutes.

He wondered whether he would get the information he sought.

Finally, after a long wait, "Yes, sir, I have what you need. Let me get your number and we will have someone contact you."

Jeff also gave the voice on the other end of the line information on where he would be for the next hour. He knew this was a hit. Now he would wait.

He didn't like to use his old contacts, since it put them in danger, so he was willing to wait for Kevin to contact him in whatever way he wanted. He suspected he would hear from him before he had time to wonder how that would be.

Jeff asked to get information on World One and Stan Fleming, including who was actually behind the organization, and what they wanted. He would also ask for traces on any calls made to Bob's phone. Then he waited patiently at Whiskey Bar, looking at his watch and then his phone in turn.

As he waited for his friend, he ran through what he already knew. Bob had been investigating World One before he was killed, and had briefed Jeff and Lil on his last meeting with Stan Flemming, the head of World One, several days before the explosion. According to Bob, this anomaly had formed seemingly overnight. Walker, Wright and Turner had been struggling to do their homework to find out what it was all about. Bob hadn't found much, though he'd come up with some information about the corporation. One thing was abundantly clear – they were petitioning against the new affirmative action bills. Project Performance was their target at the moment, and WWT was looking after that particular bill's best interests. It had brought World One and the firm into direct contact.

Jeff considered this and realized there must be a connection between Bob's death and World One. He thought through all of their other cases and nothing stood out except for this. Yet it didn't follow that a bill about diversity would put Bob and the firm at risk. Jeff knew there was a connection there and time would reveal more clues. He hoped his friend could help.

Jeff and Bob had frequented the Whiskey Bar, which was across the street from their office. It didn't look like much, but the atmosphere was perfect for an after-hours unwinding session. He sat in the bar now, staring into his drink as the memories washed over him. His deep, methodic breathing caused ripples to flow across the surface of his drink.

A tear found its way down his cheek, and he buried his face in his trembling hands. When he looked up again, he'd wiped the tear away and composed his features. He didn't have time for that kind of thing, and he knew that it wouldn't help. He had to find out who did this and why. It didn't make sense to kill over a bill – there had to be more to it. And it had to be someone crazy enough to risk it all over this piece of legislation, or someone who had nothing to lose.

He found himself staring at his reflection in the mirror behind the bar, and noticed that his hair was getting longer, his black curls now reaching to just above his collar. He could see a little 5 o'clock shadow covering his jawline, and his eyes looked tired. Very tired. He rubbed his temples, trying desperately to focus, and pulled his mind back to the business at hand.

A thick hand suddenly slapped his left shoulder, tearing him out of his thoughts. Jeff smiled, assuming that Kevin had finally arrived, and was surprised when he turned and came face to face with a stranger. The man was smiling nastily at him.

"Let's take a walk, friend." The man grabbed Jeff forcefully by the left arm and tugged. Jeff jerked his arm back, defying the strong grip of the other man, and scowled at him.

"I don't know you, *friend*," he growled, standing to face the other man.

"I think you want to hear what I have to say."

Jeff looked the man squarely in the eye, then turned to look for the bartender. No one seemed to have noticed his actions or those of the man speaking to him. Everyone was involved in some kind of drunken, animated conversation, concerned with their own lives rather than the actions of those around them.

Jeff threw his money on the bar, cursing the blindness of the masses, and led the way to the street. He turned his face into the cold and shielded his eyes from the wind, but didn't turn to face the man behind him.

"Tell me what you have to say. I have other things on my mind right now," he said coldly.

"Oh, I think I know exactly what's on your mind. Let's walk." The man had a familiar voice, but Jeff couldn't place it. "I have some information that you probably want, but nothing comes without a price," the man added, propelling Jeff forward. "Kevin sent me."

Jeff frowned. He didn't trust the man, and realized quickly that something must have gone terribly wrong. No one knew Kevin, and the fact that this man knew his name made Jeff extremely nervous. This case was starting to look a lot bigger than he had realized.

"Listen, I don't need your information, and I'm not going to wait around or pay for it. Either tell me or get out of my face." He turned and met the man nose to nose. He'd been through a lot over the last week, and nothing this man could say would move him.

"This price has no dollar sign," the man sneered. "It is a much higher price to pay." He turned away to watch the cars moving along the icy street. Steam rose through the street manholes and met the bright street lights in the distance. It gave the street an eerie, unreal feeling, and Jeff shivered.

Silence fell between the two men as they sized each other up. Jeff looked into the man's eyes and read his body language, trying to figure out who the man was and whether he was a serious threat. How did he know about Kevin? Had he hurt Kevin, or done something with him? And what did he know about Jeff's case, and Bob's death? A couple walked from the back of the bar, giggling, and strolled past them. The two men held each's gazes and barely noticed the couple as they passed.

The man waited until the couple turned the corner, then added slowly and quietly, "I know, because your friend paid that price. I'm sorry about what happened, truly. That's why I'm here. It shouldn't have happened, and I want to keep it from happening again. But I'm risking my life in telling you this.

"You have no idea what you are up against," the man continued. "Your call to Kevin put you and your firm at great risk. Kevin is ok, for now. He has gone dark in order to protect you both. He asked that I warn you. And now ... there are very powerful people who want you dead, because of the questions you've been asking."

"Who the hell are you, and what do you know about anything?" Jeff asked angrily. He was frustrated by the man's cool demeanor and accent, and the hidden threat of Bob's death only made things worse. And what about Kevin? Kevin was a professional, and rarely needed help. Few people knew that he even existed. How had this man known about him, and how were they connected?

If the man was truly here to share information, he was taking his sweet time about it, and making it awfully difficult. And there was no guarantee that he was telling the truth – he might be a mole, sent out to reel Jeff in. With that thought, Jeff shoved the man into the brick wall of a storefront, pressed an arm across his throat, and growled at him.

"Tell me what you have to say, or I'll kill you myself."

"It's simple. Things are never as they seem. If it seems too good to be true – believe me to tell the truth – it is." The man paused and seemed to measure his words as he spoke them. "I'm talking about Victoria."

"What? Who the hell are you?" Jeff muttered, pressing his arm against the man's neck.

The man shook his head slightly. "That is not important, but this is: Victoria is not as she seems. There is much that you don't know. I suggest that you look the other way, instead of walking into the trap that has already been set. I am simply a friend, trying to help."

The man finally shoved back, and Jeff fell towards the street. "You will listen to me if you want to keep what you have. She is connected to some very dark characters, Jeff. There are very important and powerful people involved, and they don't care about your life. If you look the other way, you might survive. If you don't, you will not."

The man paused.

"And forget about the search for answers on Bob's death. You won't find anything, only trouble. And one more thing ... you'd better give Holly a call."

The man turned and walked quickly down the street, into the rising mist from the manholes. After a few moments, Jeff could see only his dark silhouette against the dimly lit buildings.

He watched until even that disappeared, his mind racing. The man's words seemed to hang in the air, but they meant nothing to him. Nothing.

Suddenly he thought about what the man had said about Holly, and realized that he hadn't spoken to her since all of this started. Another thought followed quickly on the first: If he wasn't safe, she might not be safe either. Their friendship was well known, and the sort of people he was dealing with might hurt her to get to him. He replayed the conversation with the man, searching for more information, then grabbed his phone from his pocket.

As he dialed, he went through the rest of the conversation. The stranger left him with more questions than answers, whether he'd meant to or not. How did he know Victoria, and what did she have to do with anything? How had he known that Jeff knew Victoria? Jeff couldn't understand her connection at all, though he meant to ask. He felt that he would hear from this man again, though he couldn't say why ... the man had seemed sure that Jeff needed information, and had seemed to have more to share.

He finished dialing the number and waited through three rings, finally getting her voicemail. Another voicemail, he thought nervously. What was it with people not answering their phones lately? The last time someone hadn't answered their phone ... He pulled his thoughts away from Bob, refusing to think that Holly may have met the same fate. His instincts told him that all of this was connected, somehow. He just needed to figure out how. And why. The one thing he did know was that he needed to get out of here.

At the beep, Jeff simply said, "Holly, I'm on my way over."

He started walking toward his car. As he looked down, he saw the neon reflections of the bar signs on Main. Just a few blocks away was the Brooklyn, and his thoughts lingered on the last night he spent there – before any of this tragedy started. From there, his mind went back to his last afternoon with Bob.

Lost in thought, he realized he had already walked the familiar two-minute walk from the bar to his parking spot across the street. He spotted his car in the parking garage attached to his office building, and jogged across the street toward it, looking up at his building as he crossed the street.

His office light was still on.

That was odd; he always turned the lights off before he left, and if he forgot, his secretary took care of it. He thought about going up to turn off the lights, but decided against it, turning instead toward his car and the idea of home.

***

Stefano rounded the corner and thought about his warning to Jeff. He hoped he heard the message, as it was the first and last one he'd ever get from him. He took a great risk meeting Jeff, and did so only at Victoria's insistence. Al had found out about Jeff's call to his friend Kevin, and they both knew it had put him in great danger. Victoria told Al she would take care of it, hoping it would stop him from doing anything rash. He and Victoria had been surprised even then about Al's far-reaching network.

Stefano reached his destination and stopped his thoughts. He stopped and looked up at the office building in front of him and counted the floors. Time to get back to work. He reflected on the two roles he was playing, but he didn't stop long enough to let it sink in. *It pays the bills*, he thought to himself.

He walked around the building and to the side entrance that he knew would be unlocked, slipping in unnoticed and walking straight to the elevator bank. Within seconds the elevator chimed and he stepped in. Once he arrived at his floor, he exited and walked directly to the office down the hall that he had seen on the floor plans the day before. His memory was impeccable.

He pulled the key out of his pocket and slid it easily into the lock to open the door to Walker, Wright and Turner. He found Jeff's office toward the back of the space and walked directly to his desk, which he rummaged through, lights blazing throughout the office.

He needed a specific file, and he didn't have a lot of time, so he wasn't being careful. He'd already been through all of the filing cabinets he could find in the office, and the end tables around the couch.

Finding nothing in the desk, he walked over to the office clearly marked "Bob Walker," and started to open drawers of the big mahogany desk he found there. Nothing in these drawers either.

Frustrated, he looked up at the table next to the desk, and there it was. Clearly labeled, "US Industries vs. International Trade Co." Hidden in plain sight. He flipped the file open and found exactly what he'd been sent for: the list. Pulling the single page from the file, he sank slowly into the chair behind the desk and turned.

Lawyers got it pretty good, he thought to himself, taking in for a moment the luxurious office around him. He flipped on the computer and pulled a piece of paper from his back pocket, scanning it quickly. His boss was a wiz at getting information, so he shouldn't be surprised by what he saw. He shook his head, though, smiling to himself.

There, scribbled on the piece of paper, was Bob Walker's personal password, for his computer in the office.

Stefano punched it in and the computer came to life, running through a number of files and documents as it booted up. He searched the file directory for a file entitled "World One," and found it quickly. His thumb drive went into the right slot, and the file was copied in a matter of seconds. One click later, the same file was deleted from the computer's hard drive.

He smiled in satisfaction, pulled the thumb drive out, and shut down the computer. True, a computer tech could find the file again if he looked hard enough, but he'd have to know the name of the file he was looking for, and Stefano didn't think that was going to happen. He swung the chair around and walked to the window just in time to catch sight of Jeff walking to his car. The man glanced up at the office again and frowned, but then got into his car and drove away.

Stefano laughed; guy didn't even think to check why the lights were still on in his – closed – office. He wouldn't have a clue what hit him, despite the warning Stefano had delivered. He shook his head; someone needed to give Al a run for his money and at this point, he knew Jeff was the only one that could. But he needed to get a lot smarter.

He strode out slowly, catching the lights on his way and closing the door behind him. He left the office a mess, but had been careful to leave no trace or clues to his identity. The police would report a simple robbery. He'd grabbed a couple of things that looked valuable and stuffed them into his jacket, just to throw them off his scent. The secretary had kept a nice stash of money, and Jeff's office had contained a valuable Rolex, which did nicely as the reason for the robbery. He slipped the watch onto his wrist, stepped into the elevator, and knew exactly where to go next. He would be excited to see her again, though he doubted she'd feel the same.

Chapter 16

Holly closed her eyes and tried to gather her thoughts. She remembered Jack locking her in the car, but couldn't remember why he'd done it, or what had happened after. When she couldn't remember anything else, she opened her eyes to see that she was surrounded by officers and swirling colored lights. The officers were pounding on the window of the car, asking her to unlock the door. She instinctively reached to unlock the door and sat, motionless, while they opened it.

Her body seemed light as air as they carried her to an officer's squad car. She didn't have the strength to ask what had happened, but it seemed obvious that *something* had. She stared into the eyes of the unknown officers, dazed, as they peppered her with a barrage of meaningless questions. All they had were questions, and she had no answers. She would have answered them if she could, but her mind was fuzzy and vague, and she had no idea what had happened. She heard the officers call for a psyche unit, and mutter into their radios that it appeared they would need it. She didn't notice the sheet-covered body 20 feet away, or the set of skid marks leading toward the body.

Once the psyche unit arrived, they tried to explain to Holly what had happened, and even where she was. After several tries, her memory came rushing back, like a ton of bricks, and hit her in the face. She jumped to her feet and looked desperately for Jack, remembering that he had been in trouble the last time she'd seen him.

"No!" she screamed above the wailing sirens. "Jack!" She stared in horror at the covered body in the street, then collapsed to the ground.

Just then, an ambulance arrived. She found herself surrounded by EMTs asking her the same questions, and covered her head with her arms to close out the noise.

"You'd better come with us," one of them said, pulling up a stretcher.

As Holly lay down on the stretcher, looking up at the strangers' faces surrounding her, her world started to spin, and the tears began to fall. She was loaded quickly into the ambulance, one of the EMTs shielding her from the cameras of the media, and the ambulance roared to life, headed for the hospital.

***

Jeff was on his way to Holly's when he got the call. He immediately turned his car around and drove for for the hospital. No question now that this was connected; there were too many coincidences to be *real* coincidences. His thoughts drifted back to the office he'd just left, and he remembered the lights that had shown from the windows. Now he realized what those lights had meant; someone had been in the office after he'd left, and he didn't think it was his secretary. Now it looked like someone had followed Holly – and attacked her – tonight. Was it the same person? Who was behind it? And why Holly? He put away the unanswered questions for the moment, and pushed his car harder toward the hospital.

***

Officers were stationed outside of her room, and came in throughout the night to ask her questions. Questions to which she had no answers. Everything was still a blur, but as her thoughts cleared she remembered more and more about the details of the date. Halfway through the night, she remembered something important.

"That face," she whispered, reaching back into the memory of the night.

"Ma'am?" a young officer asked, confused.

"That face," she repeated, reaching for the officer at her side. "You need to find the man that was following me. He..." she trailed off, closing her eyes at the thought. "He killed Jack."

The officer looked at his supervisor, who stepped into the room. "Could you describe him?" he asked quickly.

"Yes, absolutely, every detail," she responded firmly. Her mind had already started to rebuild his face from memory. She recounted every detail that she could remember, including the make, model and color of his car.

***

Just then, Jeff arrived at her room, striding through the doorway in a rush. The officer who had been taking the description stopped him with a hand on his arm.

"She's pretty shaken up, sir," he said. "Not exactly in any shape for visitors."

Jeff continued without stopping to talk to the officer, and rushed to Holly's bedside. She teared up at the sight of him and grasped his hand.

"Oh Jeff..." she said, her voice pleading. "What is going on? Why did this happen?"

He grabbed her and held her close to him. "I'm just glad you're ok," he answered quietly, doing his best to comfort her. The fact that she'd been put in danger terrified and angered him; he never would have forgiven himself if something had happened to her.

The doctor entered and nodded, indicating that she was clear and ready to be discharged.

"I'll take her home," Jeff said without question.

He stepped outside as the nurses began detaching the monitors from Holly's arm. They walked her through the discharge paperwork and handed her several prescriptions for the pain, along with sleeping pills and sedatives to help her with the anxiety.

As the nurses saw to her discharge, Jeff stood outside the room, pumping the officers there for information.

"Who do you think did this is?" he asked the young officer next to him.

"Well sir, we got a pretty good description from her and we've sent out an APB on his whereabouts. She gave us a description of the Mustang he was driving as well, so we have roadblocks set up around the area to try to find him. We've got everyone available on this one."

The officer received a call on his radio and paused for a moment, listening. "Hey, Chief Kouros wants to talk to you sir," he said, turning back to Jeff. "He says that as long as you're here, he wants to ask you some more questions about what happened to your business partner Bob."

Jeff knew that he'd probably be on a list of possible perpetrators, now that he'd been linked to two incidents – Bob and Holly. He shook his head and knew this would be sorted out, but his first priority was to take care of his friend.

"Later, Officer," Jeff answered. "I'm taking Holly home first." He looked past the officer to see one of the nurses wheeling her out of the room. She looked up at him helplessly.

"I'll take her from here." He took the wheel chair from the nurse, who nodded and handed the paperwork and prescriptions to Holly.

"Make sure she gets those pills," she said to Jeff. "It'll help her sleep tonight. She's been pretty traumatized."

Jeff simply nodded, and pushed Holly toward the exit. He'd left his car sitting at the front entrance, and wheeled her directly to the passenger side, then helped her into the low seat.

"We're going to the pharmacy, and then straight to your house," he muttered, his mind running through all the possibilities. "I'm not taking any more chances with you." He jumped into the driver's side and slammed on the gas, squealing out of the parking lot in the direction of home.

***

When they finally entered her house, Holly heaved a sigh of relief. This, at least, was familiar, and safe. She paused, though, looking around her spotless place and trying to pinpoint what was wrong. Then it occurred to her. Every light was on, which was odd; she'd left here in mid-morning, when no lights would have been necessary. She shrugged and left them on, thinking that it would be safer; she didn't want any thoughts of the night creeping into her head. There were things that she didn't want to remember. At that thought, she looked toward Jeff.

"Thank you for coming for me, Jeff, I was so scared."

He nodded, then turned to see the police car pull up in front of the house. The young officer had told them he'd follow them over with his partner to keep an eye on things. They planned to keep a watch on Holly's house all night, in case the perpetrator had plans to harm her.

Jeff walked to the door to greet the officers.

"Sir, we need you down at the station to talk to Kouros," one of them said. "He thinks that these two situations might be connected. We'll keep an eye on Holly from here, sir."

"I'll be fine, Jeff, really. Help these guys find out who did this," Holly said, sounding as confident as she could. She knew they needed his help. "Really, I'm fine. Just keep your phone on. I'll call you if I need anything."

She struggled to maintain her composure. On the inside she wanted to scream and beg Jeff not to leave her side. Her thoughts were racing to the point she had difficulty focusing, and she was terrified. But if he could help them find the man responsible, that was more important than staying here to make her feel better.

He pulled his phone out of his pocket and glanced at it, then put it back. "You got it. It's on, and I've got the volume set as loud as it'll go. You sure you're ok?" he asked, concerned.

"I'm fine. These officers are going to take good care of me."

The young officer smiled back at Holly. "Yes, sir, we'll take good care of her for you." He walked back outside to the car with his partner, giving Jeff and Holly a moment to say goodbye.

Jeff gave Holly a big hug and she nestled into his arms, trying to memorize the feeling of safety there. She didn't want him to go, but also knew that this was the best bet at catching the guy who had been following her. Jeff was always coming to her rescue, and he also had a way of knowing more than he realized when it came to important situations. If they could catch the man, then she could relax, and that was what she needed.

"Call me if you need anything – anything at all." He stood back and walked toward the door, then turned around to glance at her again. "Anything. I mean it."

Holly nodded and watched him walk out to his car. Her heart sank lower as he backed slowly out of the driveway and headed toward the police station. When he was out of sight, she turned and walked back into the house, shutting the door firmly behind her.

***

The night lasted forever. Every few hours, Holly saw the reflection of another black and white patrol car driving past her house. The floor-to-ceiling windows didn't block out much of the activity from the street, and she felt better knowing that those men were out there watching after her.

As she sat, she replayed the night in her mind, looking for clues. The face popped back into her mind, and she flinched. Who was he? Why was he interested in her? Why had he killed Jack?

She looked at the bottle of pills the hospital doctor had prescribed for sleep. She wasn't into taking medication, no matter how much she needed it, so she set the bottle down on the table in her kitchen, and walked back to her bedroom to change into her pajamas. Finally crawling into bed, she settled in for the long rest of the night. But her mind raced through the events of the last few hours, busy trying to solve the puzzle. Who would do this? Why?

She shut her eyes to try to block out the thoughts. When she opened them, she could see headlights washing the room in light, even briefly, and was comforted knowing there were officers keeping an eye on her. She closed her eyes again and thought about Jeff and all he had done for her. She recalled a memory of her, Sidney and Jeff headed to the lake to meet some of their other friends. She was safe.

She took a deep breath and savored the fun memory as she drifted off to sleep.

Chapter 17

"Lily, hi, Jeff here. Yeah, I need you to make sure someone goes and checks out our offices in Dallas." He listened to her affirmative response. "But don't go yourself. Someone was there tonight. The office lights were on and I know none of us left them on. I distinctly remember leaving last and turning the lights off." He paused again, listening to her response.

"I'm headed to the police station right now, to talk to the chief about Bob's case. I'll ask one of the officers to head to the office as well. In fact, wait for me to call. Just steer clear of the office and lay low for now, stay out of sight. Someone is out there looking for us, and until we know who it is, we'd best just stay out of sight."

Lil was still in her hotel in Dallas, and Jeff felt that she'd be safe there. He hung up the phone, hoping that he was right. He didn't know what he'd do if something happened to her as well.

As he drove, he tried to make a list of all the people who might want them dead, and why. Nothing made any sense, though; this killer – or set of killers – was cloaked in darkness, and they weren't leaving any trails. As he thought about the threat to his friends and partners, though, he became angrier and angrier. With his anger came a sharper clarity of mind. *Everyone leaves a trail*, he thought. Even professionals revealed themselves eventually, if someone was waiting and watching for them. The next time, Jeff promised himself, he would be there to get them

Chapter 18

Jeff arrived at the police station just after 11:30 p.m. The place was quiet, with a few overweight officers grabbing sandwiches out of the vending machine and eating them at their desks. It reeked of stale smoke and salami. He had just started to walk to the back, where he saw a door marked "Chief Kouros," when a gruff voice snarled at him.

"You can't go back there," it said.

Jeff ignored the voice and kept walking, but stopped when a meaty hand fell hard on his shoulder, stopping him in his tracks.

"The name's Jeff Walker," he snarled, whirling toward the hand. "You know, of Walker, Wright and Foster. If you guys were doing your job I wouldn't have to be down here. Now, would you like to remove your hand and try again? And how about a little nicer tone?"

The man drew back, but didn't take his hand from Jeff's shoulder. "Listen, buddy, I don't know who you think you are, but this here is a police station–" His voice started to elevate, and he lowered his brows.

Just then, though, Chief Kouros rushed up to squelch the potential conflict. "Hey, guys, settle down. I got it, Mike."

"I can take care of this guy," Mike snarled, still staring directly at Jeff.

"Jeff, Chief Kouros," Kouros said, extending his thick hand toward Jeff. Jeff took it slowly, nodding at the chief. "Let's go to my office, Jeff." He turned back to his officer. "I got it. Go back to your dinner and settle down, Mike."

Chief Kouros' office was at the end of the hall, past the center corral of officer desks. When Jeff entered, he saw that the office was small but tidy, with a few awards and trophies adorning the walls.

Chief Kouros closed the door and motioned for Jeff to take a seat in the burnt orange vinyl seat opposite his desk. Kouros himself slumped into his chair.

"Well, you certainly know how to make an entrance." Kouros eyed Jeff and tried to lighten the mood, but his attempts went unnoticed. Jeff stared blankly back at Kouros, waiting for the interview to begin.

"Okay, let's get right to it then," Kouros sighed. "Jeff, when was the last time you saw Bob alive?" He twirled his long, peppered mustache, waiting for Jeff's answer.

"I think I've already been through this with your officers," Jeff answered. "I saw him in the office on Friday. We had a meeting on the Giovani case, which lasted until 6:30 p.m. We decided we'd discuss it more in depth that evening, and broke for dinner. I went out for dinner with a friend. I thought Bob could handle the client – he usually does. I saved the tape. It just doesn't make any sense." Jeff's head dropped.

Kouros nodded. "You told me he called you that night. What did he say?"

Jeff recited what he could remember about the conversation, while Kouros took notes. "I made a phone call in the afternoon to help dig up some information on Al Chord's organization, International Exchange Company, and I asked him to do some more research about Stan Flemming, who runs World One. He'd already been handling that particular case, and I thought that he was the best one to dig for more info. We had won a case for an audit of Al's company, and it led us to World One. We learned through our own investigation that Al and Stan seemed to know each other pretty well, and were perhaps even working together on some common interests. The phone calls, everything, started happening after we won that case and started doing research." He paused, looking at Kouros. "I don't believe in coincidences, Chief."

"Hell of a puzzle here," Kouros added. "I did some more digging myself, and you're right. There's a connection between Al and Stan, though it's very cleverly hidden. I found dollars from Al's company landing in Stan's bank account through some highly suspicious transactions, some heavy laundering going on between. Big amounts of money. Got me to thinking ... what if these boys are doing business together, and what exactly are trying to hide?"

"Well, let's get to the bottom of it, then."

"My thoughts exactly." Kouros paused, then smiled grimly. "What do you say we pay Stan Flemming a little visit?"

Chapter 19

Al paced back and forth in heightened agitation. Gordon knew to stay silent at times like this; he kept to the back of the room and watched the scene unfold. He could see the sweat, even from this distance, glistening on Stefano's upper lip. Stefano didn't let his emotions show, but he didn't have to. All three men knew that he should be scared shitless – he had screwed up, and was in big trouble.

Al stopped pacing in front of Stefano just long enough to breathe a puff of smoke into his face. "Nice work," Al said, his smile hard as ice. "Real fuckin' nice work." He drifted back to his pacing pattern, thinking hard through the situation, and continued the speech to himself.

"A real professional, she says," he continued at a slower, more methodical pace. "We're both professionals, she says." He turned back to the man in question and spat through his grimace. "Tell me, pro, what were you thinking? Better yet, what were you thinking *with*? I'll bet Victoria is real proud of you. By the way, where is she? She'll be real interested in these new developments."

This was Gordo's clue. He rose swiftly and left the room to retrieve Victoria from one of the locked bedrooms. When they entered the den, Gordo threw her into the room. She fell hard into Al, who immediately threw her to the tile floor. She leapt to her feet, attemptig to maintain her composure in the face of the mistreatment, and wiped the blood from her lip. Stefano tried to help her, but Al swung a recently acquired pool stick at him, catching him in the groin. He doubled and fell to the ground.

"Not so fast, lover boy." Al smiled at the woman in front of him. "So what do I do with you?" he asked, sneering.

She recoiled from Al's reach.

"Not so fast, darling. You need me." He grabbed her head and pulled her toward him, then pushed his lips against hers. She stood her ground and didn't make a sound. Finally he pulled away and laughed. "That's more like it, honey." He swatted her on the butt and then winked at her. "Why don't you go put on something nice for me tonight?"

Stefano lay on the floor, crumpled into a pile, and Al glanced at him. "I'll deal with you later, Gordo get him out of here." He turned back to Victoria. "Your man screwed up, darling. Good thing I'm there for you." He turned to Victoria and rubbed his hand along her arm, smiling, then turned to walk out of the room, leaving Victoria and Stefano alone, Stefano staring at the floor.

Chapter 20

Lil did the only thing she could to keep a hold of her sanity: she worked. She found herself confined back in an office at the Dallas branch of Walker, Wright and Turner, and had plenty to keep her busy. Between her pager, her cell phone, and her e-mail, she was always accessible, and people knew it. The world had not stopped for Lil to mourn. For the moment, she was thankful; it gave her something to keep her mind off of what had happened to Bob.

Today she began with an hour-long conference call, arranged by her trusty office assistant. George had assembled a few congressmen who knew a little about the new political group on the scene, World One.

Lil mouthed the word to herself, wondering what the hell the organization wanted, and how far they were willing to go to get it. Of course, they claimed that they weren't a political group at all – merely a citizen's group interested in raising funds for Young America and any other organization that positively affected the lives of the country's youth. But Lil had heard Stan Flemming, the leader of the organization, talk, and he sure sounded like a politician.

Then there was the mystery around the membership. She suspected that the membership mirrored the little black book Stan had brought with him from the corporate world. World One was meticulous about their paperwork, however, and Lil's office had been unable to dig up any suspicious documents or information. They knew for a fact that the organization was trying to block the bill, though, and that brought with it the question: Why would an organization that supported young Americans be interested in an equality bill? Lil fully intended to uncover this little tidbit of information.

She knew that the firm was attracting unwanted attention, and she was worried about what had happened to Bob, but that didn't mean she was going to stop doing her job. If anything, she felt that she owed it to Bob's memory. To prove that he hadn't died in vain. She looked down at the paper in front of her, reading from the bio of Stan Flemming.

Apparently, Stan Flemming had been born and raised on the lifeblood of big corporate conglomerates. He was a low-profile business manager who had risen from the rank of employee to finally become the CEO of a large high-tech company. He was spotless; a small, rather unassuming man who sported a toupee about two shades too dark for the remaining tufts of hair that peered out helplessly from each side of his head. His voice, however, was unmistakably commanding. When Stan Flemming talked, people listened, and this was beginning to annoy Lil Turner.

Stan Flemming had started the new organization a year after his retirement from corporate America, at age fifty-five. He certainly wasn't hurting for money, but it still seemed strange to Lil that he had retired at such an early age *and* begun a non-profit group in the name of America's youth. She pulled up a file on World One and read, for probably the one-hundredth time, the bio Stan had provided to the press. Other than a few inactive honorary board memberships, Stan hadn't shown a real interest in non-profit organizations pre-World One. She thought about this for a minute, and her suspicions grew.

She set the file down and pulled her laptop from her bag, which she'd slung on the arm of Jeff's office couch. She'd found her own office here to be a glorified storage facility, and had promptly taken up permanent residence in a corner of Jeff's office. Jane, his office manager, was gracious and accommodating. She'd had their IT group run a network cable for Lil so that she could set up her lifeline to DC. Lil was impressed with Jane's get-it-done attitude, and wished her own staff could be taught the same.

With one snap of the cord into the computer, Lil was ready to access the wonderful world of e-mail. She often marveled at the wonders of technology, and couldn't remember how she'd worked prior to e-mail, texting, faxing, and all the amazing gadgets of business today. How did they ever get anything done? She punched the 'receive' button on her mailbox, then stood and stretched while her e-mail files downloaded; she'd left DC several days earlier and ignored her e-mail since then, for the most part. This meant over one hundred new messages, she saw.

She groaned and turned to the panoramic view of downtown Dallas. The floor-to-ceiling windows made the view even more impressive. The sensation of looking out the window was like peering out of a moving glass elevator, she thought. She spun around, testing the sensation, and that same feeling begin to rise in the pit of her stomach. She'd been afraid of heights since she was a child, but did her best to fight through it. Now, though, the thought of nothing but glass between her and thirty floors to the pavement made her woozy.

She turned away from the windows, swallowing heavily; time to check e-mails.

"Good grief," she exclaimed, glancing at the growing list of incoming mail.

Jane popped her head in, as if on cue. "You okay in here?" she asked pleasantly. "Can I help you with anything else?"

Lil responded slowly, still shocked by the sheer number of messages. "No thanks, Jane, go ahead to lunch, I'll be fine here."

One by one, she began scanning her messages. The ones that looked less important, she printed for later reading. She had some unopened e-mails from Bob, though, and these made her pause. How could she have missed these? she wondered. The first message was an update on World One. Bob had been not only shrewd, but also incredibly resourceful. Lil wiped a stray tear from her cheek, then closed her eyes briefly and swallowed hard. He would have done a lot of research, and this message would probably contain that. It would also be the last time she received a message from him.

She printed the message and continued through her e-mails, trying to move forward with the job. Some were from other lawyers on the same path of suspicion as Lil and Walker, Wright and Turner. She had started to build a network of attorneys personally interested in seeing the success of Project Performance. All lawyers, at least the good ones, dedicated part of their time to pro-bono work, and Project Performance had become Lil's passion. She'd made sure that she wasn't the only lawyer on the case. In fact, her contributions had led to wide media coverage that directly benefited her firm. Soon after her involvement began, client referrals went way up. Jeff had been forced to handle the larger cases and begin bringing in young lawyers to alleviate some of their case overload. The young ones could do most of the footwork, while Lil, Bob and Jeff had handled the heavy lifting.

Project Performance was a pro-bono case that the firm had taken on at the insistence of Lil Turner, and now that small pet project had immersed the firm in a web of danger. The project had therefore led to more money and publicity for the firm, becoming one of their most important projects. It had also, though, been one of their most tragic.

As she scrolled down, she found another message from Bob, this one marked urgent and coded confidential. WWT had a system of passwords and codes to ensure confidentiality of some of their most sensitive information, but Lil was surprised to see it here. She pulled her organizer out to find the password for Bob's e-mail. She flipped right to it; the page in her address book marked for Bob was dog-eared and worn from years of frequent use.

The password was buried in his address to throw the casual snoop off track: "Maverick." Bob loved the Dallas Mavericks and they had been to many games. She smiled at the memory, then set down the address book and began slowly typing in the code. She hit enter cautiously, her stomach turning over as the computer began to whir with a response, and took a deep breath as the screen began to fill. What she saw shocked her.

"Oh my God," she involuntarily gasped, examining the information before her. She turned and grabbed the phone, intent on calling Jeff with this new information.

Chapter 21

Al loved to watch Victoria and Stefano sweat. He needed them around a little longer, but he wasn't about to let them know that. The police would begin an investigation, but the description of the Mustang Stefano was driving or even the license plate would be worthless. The car was a rental that Gordo had stolen from some poor tourist at their hotel parking lot during the night. By the next morning, the poor slob would report that it was stolen, but Gordo had already driven it from Austin to Dallas. The car was long gone, and the report of the stolen car wouldn't make it here in time.

He also knew that the description of Stefano would be virtually useless. Though he seemed to be careless this time, he had been trained by the best. His disguises were undetectable and completely untraceable. And beyond that, he was an import. This was the first time Al had used him, though he came with high marks from Victoria, who had used him many times in other regions.

Al smiled and nodded to Gordo, who grabbed Victoria's arm and marched her back to the locked room. Divide and conquer, Al thought to himself.

He paused to admire Victoria.

"Nice dress," he said, noticing she had cleaned herself up and put on a tight-fitting red dress.

To anyone who knew him in the United States, Al Chord was nothing more than a shrewd businessman. He had studied the English language, American customs, American history, and even American culture for years so that he would fit in here. To the untrained eye and ear, he seemed like just another American, whose parents had perhaps brought him to America, the land of opportunity. He'd worked hard to gain an American accent as well, with a Northeastern slant.

In reality, he had been to the Northeast only briefly. He'd spent most of his years in Texas, with frequent visits to Washington, DC, under the guise of business. In fact, his money had been spread throughout greedy pockets in Washington, DC. And Al always got a good deal for his money.

Ten years ago, he'd started his own textile business. The company produced fabric for nearly 80 percent of the top Texas designers. And with NAFTA, he had become a major importer of Mexican weave fabrics. His textile business supplied over 40% of the product that ended up in home furnishings across the United States. Al served on many major business boards, and, to the naked eye, appeared to be on the up and up.

He was pretty popular in the community as well, having been voted by two major magazine audiences as one of Dallas' most eligible bachelors. That wasn't in the original plan, but Al wasn't about to disappoint all those women. One of the other recipients had been none other than Jeff Michael Walker. Both men took the award in stride and used it to bolster their respective businesses. Al used it as a way to boost his image of good businessman doing good deeds.

Jeff's nomination was the first time that Al had noticed the other man. Since then they had spent time on various boards together and mingled at many social events, and knew each other loosely as business connections.

Al was known for his slick, distinguished looks, dark brown eyes, and predominately dark features. His skin was a smooth satin olive, and he had straight, dark hair that he pushed back for that "I just walked off Wall Street" look. Jeff was the diametric opposite of Al, which had always seemed ironic to the businessman. The lawyer was known primarily for his rugged good looks and charm, from his chiseled jaw to his loose but well-fitted suits, his 6'2" frame, and the look of the entire package. The two bachelors posed for both magazine covers during the voting, and their professional careers had crossed more than once. Al knew more about Jeff than he knew about his own father.

Jeff had first represented Al in a trade dispute against another textile company in Texas. The case had been swift and easy, but Al had watched Jeff intently. Jeff didn't know he was being studied for future use.

Al had a good reason for watching the other man, and a plan for what to do with him. He'd planned to hire Jeff and his firm to represent him in another trade dispute. He would use this as an opportunity to see how he operated, and find out if he could use him in his plan. His friends in Cuba alerted him to Jeff's clandestine past and his time as an agent. He knew much about many people. Al's network through World One also afforded him great access and information on most everyone. Jeff was no different. Yet even Al's network of intelligence only went so far, and Al knew in order to stay truly informed you kept your friends close, and your enemies closer.

Chapter 22

Victoria sat slowly on the edge of the bed, and watched as Gordo closed and locked the door between them. She knew that it was only for the appearance as she looked down at the key that Gordo had just slipped into her hand. His resolve to protect Al was starting to wane as his affection for Victoria grew, and he was now showing a sense of chivalry. She fingered the key in her hand; this was her ticket to freedom.

There were only two windows in this room, overlooking the lit pool one floor down. Al's "security team" was visible at all corners of the expansive garden, so escape was out of the question. She looked around the room, which was sparsely decorated. The pieces that were there, however, were obviously valuable – antiques, she thought, impressed.

She walked to the window and surveyed the back yard, which resembled more of a public garden. The house was situated on a large 5-acre lot – almost unheard of in this exclusive neighborhood just north of downtown Dallas – but Al had paid good money for the privacy and space.

From this window, she could see parts of the winding driveway before it disappeared around the bend toward the front door. She watched as a car wound around the long drive.

"Hm, company," she said to herself. She wondered who was here, and whether Al was expecting them. She was smarter than Al realized, and knew that he needed her. She also knew she wouldn't live to see her thirtieth birthday if she didn't find a way out of this room. She had planned for this event, though; a plan she'd always considered an insurance policy, in case of disaster.

She had been in some precarious positions before, and had designed some pretty amazing escapes, learning from each situation and teaching herself more as time went on. The alluring but conservative persona she portrayed to the public was only one side of her character. The darker side took her deep into an unknown and seductive world of lies and betrayal.

It wasn't the money that brought her, although that was nice. It was the thrill of leading double lives. She'd found a home in the intelligence field, and had moved deeper from there into the clandestine role she played today. The risk of staying uncover for too long was the risk of being lost in the character. There were guidelines about how long to keep operatives under cover, and she knew she was near that line of no return. She became addicted to the lies, and the lines began to blur. Her husband had never understood this dark pull, and hadn't liked that she'd put her life in danger again and again. He didn't like that she'd had to keep secrets from him, either, and it had eventually led to her divorce. This only took her further into the darkness.

The lights from the car disappeared behind the west wing of the house.

She looked down at her phone and saw the text. *At police station.* She reached for her purse and threw the phone in, along with her red lipstick, then walked back to the window and peered out at the parade of cars.

She knew that Al's plan was falling into place, and that his associates were beginning to show for their last meeting before the big event. This also meant that Al would be busy. He would expect her to leave, to take care of some loose ends, and wouldn't send anyone after her if he found her gone. This was, after all, part of their unspoken agreement; they both pretended that he was in charge, and that she was at his mercy.

They both knew, though, that she was capable of leaving at any point.

She looked down and opened her hand, revealing the small key that Gordo had given her. It hadn't taken much digging to find his soft spot, or learn that he disagreed with how Al treated her. From there, it had been a quick step to taking advantage of him.

Without another thought, she let herself out of the room and slipped past the front door to the car waiting for her in the front drive.

***

Jeff and Kouros exited the police station around midnight. They shook hands, Kouros agreeing to keep Jeff up to date on their findings.

"Don't be a vigilante, these guys don't mess around," he warned Jeff. "Go home and get some rest. Let's chat in the morning."

Jeff nodded and then walked to his car, parked under the bright light to the right of the parking lot. He slid in and powered up the Porsche, gripping the steering wheel and taking a deep breath. He could sense that things were unraveling and wondered where the threads would lead. Who else was in danger? How was Holly?

He reached into his pocket and found his phone. He looked at the screen and decided since it was so late he'd send Holly a text. *Just left police station. You ok?* That done, he set the phone down and headed toward home.

As he drove, he reflected again on the threads of information he had so far: the connection between Bob and his investigation into World One, the threats connected to Project Performance, and Stan Flemming. It was time they learned more about him. He and Kouros had planned to go by his office this week and ask a few questions.

He didn't know though if they had that kind of time.

***

Victoria watched from a car parked in the other side of the street. When Jeff was several blocks ahead, she leaned forward toward the driver's seat. "Driver, follow that Porsche," she muttered quietly.

They wound their way through the neighborhood streets, staying a good distance behind the Porsche, and finally arriving at their destination. Victoria's driver parked a block away and she watched as Jeff pulled into his driveway, opened up his garage, and drove in, closing the door immediately behind him.

The driver pulled up slowly, watching the house as the lights began turning on from room to room. He looked back at Victoria, shrugging.

"Well?"

"Wait," she said.

She turned to the passenger on her right, her voice growing firmer. "Just tell him what you know." She waited until she received a nod, then turned back toward Jeff's house.

The driver pulled the car forward to the driveway, and Victoria and her passenger got slowly out of the car. It was a dark night, providing good cover for discretion.

She leaned over to the driver's window. "Go around the block. I'll text you when we're ready." The driver nodded and left to drive up and around the block.

"Let's go," she told the man next to her. She led the way to Jeff's door, knocking lightly when she got there. A few moments later, the porch light came on and she grimaced, not wanting to be noticed by Jeff's neighbors. They were taking a tremendous risk.

Then the door flew open, revealing Jeff's shocked face. "It's you!" he said incredulously. He looked over to Victoria's right, and saw Stan Flemming standing there.

His face became steel. Looked like he wouldn't be paying Stan Flemming a visit after all. The man had come to *him*; another thread.

"Hurry, Jeff, let us in. It's not safe for us to be out here."

Jeff led them into his living room, then turned. "Well, this is certainly a surprise. So you two know each other?"

He looked at the odd pair standing before him in his living room, falling silent as he digested the apparent connection between Victoria and Stan Flemming. He motioned toward the couches in his living room just beyond the entryway of his house.

"Well, why don't we sit down for a minute?"

"We don't have time for that. In fact, we don't have much time at all, Jeff. Stan here needs to tell you some things. Stan..." She turned toward the businessman expectantly, waiting for him to get started.

The three continued to stand stoically in the living room, and Stan began. "I work with Al Chord. I believe you, your colleagues, and friends have been having a bit of trouble

143

lately. There's more to it than you realize. You're all in great danger. I'm risking my life to tell you this."

He paused and looked at Victoria, knowing that she was in great danger too. His eyes darted around the room nervously.

Jeff watched and thought he could see a twitch developing over this guy's left eye. He could almost see a slight tremor in his left hand. Both of those things meant he was nervous, and that he was indeed telling the truth. He was truly terrified to be doing it.

"I met Al Chord many years ago. He asked that I run a non-profit business for him, called World One. But I can tell you that this business is anything but non-profit. And Al Chord has ideas – terrible plans. It's gotten out of hand, and I know that I'm partially to blame. But I didn't know he would take it this far. He's arranging something terrible and you need to be careful. Don't go digging too deeply." Stan's words hung in the air, unfinished.

"Wait a minute, Stan, slow down and tell me what you're talking about. Are you saying that Al is at the center of things? Is he connected in some way to what happened to my friends? What are you saying Stan, I'm not following," Jeff said sternly. "Are you saying he's after me?"

"In a word, yes," Stan said, his eyes darting toward the windows. He slowly backed up against the wall by the door.

***

Victoria watched as Stan Flemming began to sweat. She realized the man was likely to have a nervous breakdown and grabbed his arm to bring him back. *Not now*, she thought, *not now.*

Finally, Jeff asked, "So, Stan, what is it you think I should do?"

"Stan, tell him what you know. He can likely help," she urged, still watching the beads of sweat forming on his brow. *He may not make it*, she thought. He was a good front man, but didn't have much in the way of a spine.

"Al is meeting tonight with his organization. I'm due back there soon, to be a part of this meeting. Once he puts things in motion, it will be difficult to stop. He's been smuggling weapons into this country for many years, disguised in textiles shipments from Mexico. And the dockworkers are paid to look the other way. He has a large number of weapons already here, and those are just the ones I know about. I should have stopped this sooner, but I'm doing what I can now. You need to know who you're up against."

"Why are you telling me this now?" Jeff asked.

"Jeff, this has just gone too far. People are losing their lives, and more are going to die. Our way of life is now threatened. I may not have the best morals in the country, but I am a patriot. Al has far-reaching power, and he needs to be stopped. It's probably too late for us, but you can help."

Victoria grabbed Jeff's hand. Jeff looked down and held her hand for a long moment.

She leaned over and kissed him on the cheek, then whispered in his ear, "Maybe if things were different."

Her breath lingering lightly in his ear, and he shivered. She leaned closer, wondering what would happen if she gave in to her instincts. She'd been waiting to talk to this man privately for so long, and now it looked like he may be their best hope for survival. Maybe...

Suddenly Stan cleared his throat, breaking into the intimate moment. "Victoria, it's time. If we don't leave soon, Al will know that we were gone." He walked toward the door, his back to the couple standing in the living room.

Jeff turned to Victoria and stroked her hair lightly with his free hand. His other hand still grasped hers tightly. "Yes," he said simply.

She leaned in toward him and kissed him lightly on the lips, feeling a rush of emotions surging up from some unknown place, then pulled away.

She smiled slightly, then shook her head. "We've got to go. Jeff, please be careful." She released his hand and walked over to join Stan at the front door.

Stan turned back to Jeff. "Jeff, you need to know. Al Chord has lined the pockets of everyone who is anyone across government and big corporations. It will be hard to trust anyone. Watch your back."

Victoria watched Jeff's face, then realized that time was running short, and took her phone from her purse to text her driver.

Moments later, headlights lit up Jeff's front window. Victoria and Stan darted out the front door to their nondescript black car. Within seconds they were driving through the darkened night, on their way back to Al's house.

***

Jeff stood inside the front door, watching them drive away.

The lines of the good guys and bad guys were beginning to blur. Victoria and Stan were working with Al, but they had showed up on his doorstep to help him, with important information and contacts. Jeff was a man who functioned best with facts and a plan, and he had neither of those things at the moment. This was uncertain at best, and he still didn't know what he was dealing with. Al Chord was planning something diabolical? What could it possibly be? And how was he going to achieve it? He was meeting with his associates now? What were they meeting about?

Most importantly, what did this have to do with him, and how had Bob been pulled into it?

Chapter 23

Holly opened her eyes and blinked while she adjusted to the low light in her living room. For a blissful second she remained dazed from sleep. Then reality rushed back to her like an unforgiving and swift lightning bolt striking from the black night sky. She looked at the watch she had placed on the table in front of her.

It was 2 a.m. Where was Jeff?

She jumped to her feet and rushed to the window. She could see the police car parked across the street, and make out a silhouette of two figures inside the car. They appeared to be talking and sipping on a beverage. The cops were still watching the house, then, which meant that she was safe. She hoped. She let the curtain fall back over the glass and walked to her kitchen.

The events of the night before were still blurry. She only remembered snapshots of police swarming around her, dinner, the game. She grabbed a pan, oil, and popcorn to fix a late-night snack, since she knew that she hadn't eaten recently. Then she screamed.

"That face!" she gasped. She dropped the bowl, which shattered loudly on the floor. Staring back at her from the window above the sink, only 2 feet from her was the face ... the same face that had watched her at the hockey game, and then again at the restaurant.

The face of the man that had killed Jack.

Holly ran over the sharp shards from the broken bowl, desperate to get out of the kitchen and trailed blood across the light beige carpet as she headed frantically toward the door. The shatter of more glass breaking rang out from the kitchen, and she shrieked as she desperately felt her way through the dark room. She stumbled into the living room table and fell, groaning as she felt her legs buckle. Her right leg wouldn't move when she tried to pull herself up from the table, and pain ripped through her body when she tried to put weight onto her leg, so she fell helplessly to the floor again.

Pushing herself up with every ounce of strength in her body, she tried to use her arms to drag herself toward the front door, and made it several feet before she gave up. It was no use; she would tire too quickly this way, and she'd never be able to get away from her attacker.

She looked behind her, toward the kitchen, to judge how much time she had. The face was climbing through the broken glass of her back window. Only 10 feet separated them now. Turning her back on him, she clawed at the carpet, dragging herself desperately for the door.

***

Jeff was still standing in his house in the front entryway, the door still wide open.

The pieces were starting to come together, though. Al Chord had a plan. Victoria and Stan were in it together, but had now had a change of heart. Bob had lost his life as part of it, which meant that he must have found something linking back to all of this. Or had he? How was it all connected? What exactly was he missing? Jeff racked his brain, going swiftly back through everything he knew.

He had talked to Kouros *ad nauseum* about WWT's current client list, convicted parties, potential enemies, and contributors, knowing that any one of them – or a combination – could be behind Bob's death and the latest incident with Holly. They had both agreed that it had to be someone powerful calling the shots. Someone with access and means ... that could certainly be Al Chord. But how did this connect to his friend Kevin?

Though these incidents could be seen as random and not connected, he wondered now how far-reaching Al Chord's power was, and whether it could have endangered even his friend at the NSA. Could Kevin be at risk? He knew that reaching out to his old network at the NSA was risky, but he'd never thought that Al had such a far reach.

He remembered the warning from the man at the bar. Who was he? How did he know Kevin? How were all of these threads connected? He knew the answers were there, if he just slowed down and thought about each fact and narrowed down the possibilities of who could be behind this.

Though he had contacted Kevin, he never told anyone else. At this point, he wasn't entirely sure that the police had things under control. He certainly didn't know who he could trust. Now he was glad that he'd withheld some information during his conversation with Kouros. It might have saved some lives.

He hadn't told the chief about Lil's activities on Project Performance, though he still couldn't see any potential connection. Kouros and one of his officers took notes diligently throughout the interview, and it seemed like they asked the same set of questions over and over. Were the police just walking him in circles while their friends on the dark side were carrying out their plan with Al?

Jeff finally closed his door, and looked around the house that had been his home for over ten years. Suddenly he felt a pang of regret, realizing that he'd left Holly alone, when he'd promised to look after her. This wasn't where he was supposed to be. He reached for his phone in his pocket and found a text from Holly. *Not sleeping. How did it go with the police?*

He strode quickly back to the kitchen, texting that he'd be over as he walked, and found his keys sitting on the counter. He grabbed them and headed out to the garage, opening the door and flipping off the house lights. With one click of his remote the Porsche came to life. The lights came on and the driver door unlocked. He slid in and placed the car in reverse, listening to the engine roar. It was Bob who had talked him into buying the Porsche; Jeff had planned to trade in his 100,000-mile Volvo for an Audi, but he was glad he'd strayed from his typically conservative side. The Porsche was worth the extra expense. The convenience of having the car running when he got in, and the extra speed ... both were certainly coming in handy now.

He reminisced for a minute, sitting quietly in the car, and letting the memories wash over him. Every Saturday, he and Bob had headed out for at least a half-day of golf. They'd used the opportunity to catch up on events and unwind from work. Bob had always had one half of his mind on Lil, though, so they'd talked about her and their relationship as well. The thought of Lil made Jeff think about how much this situation must be tearing her apart. He knew that she would just force herself deeper into the work to try to forget, and probably need him more than ever when she came out.

That brought him back to Holly. He wanted to keep her safe, and he wasn't sure that he'd be able to do so. He knew, though, that the best start was to go be close to her, instead of on the other side of town, daydreaming.

Suddenly he noticed that the night had gone still, and put the car into gear. *Time to get out of here*, he thought, instinctively pulling into the twenty-minute drive to her house.

He'd demanded that Kouros check with the officers stationed outside Holly's residence, but they had repeatedly reported no movement or suspicious activity. They had walked the property several times, ensuring that all access points to the house were secure, and hadn't seen anything suspicious. This set Jeff's mind at ease, but he was still anxious to see her for himself and make sure that she was okay.

He finally pulled onto Holly's winding street and revved the engine. The trees were still and the full moon lit the block ahead of him brightly. He'd been driving this street for years, but had no idea who else lived on the block. His friend traveled a lot with her job as a political consultant, so was rarely at home and had never had a chance to meet many of her neighbors. Jeff had never liked this – it meant that she lived alone, surrounded by people who didn't know her. People who wouldn't help her if she was in trouble. The thought had always bothered him.

He neared the end of the street and glanced at the front of the parked police car; it looked rather conspicuous, but he was certainly glad it was there. As he neared the car, though, he began to feel an anxious knot in the pit of his stomach. Something wasn't quite right. There didn't appear to be any movement in the car. Jeff peered into the car as he drove passed it, heading toward Holly's driveway, and gasped when he saw the driver of the car.

The man was staring back at him with empty eyes, his head slumped clumsily against the driver's side window of the car. The light from the moon revealed the gory scene in vivid detail. The two officers both sat leaning against their doors and windows, staring blankly ahead. The officer sitting in the driver's seat had clearly been struck in the neck by a bullet; it had left a splattering of blood along his right side and across the dash and front windshield. The officer on the other side was slumped over, and looked as though he'd been hit in the chest.

Jeff struggled for breath and frantically looked around the street, yards, and houses for anyone or anything that could have done this. He remembered the phone he'd left carelessly on the passenger seat of the car, and fumbled now to find it. He punched 911, then squealed into Holly's driveway and glanced up.

The house was dark except for one faint light that appeared to be coming from the kitchen. Jeff swung the car door open and leaped out of the car with the cell phone still tightly grasped in his right hand; the 911 operator hadn't picked up yet, and that was his lifeline. He ran to the door and practically fell against the front entrance, yelling for Holly.

When no answer came from the house, he beat on the door loudly, unconcerned about slumbering neighbors. He reached for his keys and realized they were still in the car's ignition.

At this point, the emergency operator finally answered.

"Help me, damn it," Jeff muttered, struggling to hold the phone and grab for his keys. "There are two officers dead and I don't know what the hell happened to Holly." He fumbled the keys out of the ignition and ran back toward the front door.

"Sir, please slow down and give me your address."

"6424 Highland Park Drive. God, I hope I'm not too late. You've got to send someone now, five minutes may be too late."

The woman on the other end of the line cleared her throat. "Did you say officers down, sir?" There was a slight pause.

"Yes," Jeff responded, almost swallowing his words.

"They're on their way, sir."

Jeff sorted through his keys, the phone still pressed to one ear, and found the key to Holly's house. He shoved it into the door and thrust it open, then ran through the house. The front room was too dark to see anything, so he ran for the light in the kitchen. He saw the broken bowl on the ground, and looked up to the broken window.

"Holly!" he screamed in desperation. He looked down and noticed the blood spatters on the carpet, leading into the living room. "Oh, my God," he exclaimed. He ran through the entire house, screaming for her, then sprinted upstairs, to check her bed. When that was empty he raced back toward the living room, hitting a light switch on the way down.

He turned the corner and stopped in shock, his face horrified at what he saw.

Chapter 24

Al had a full schedule today. His assistant had him
booked solid – he had a conference call in the morning with the
United Textile Manufacturers Union, a short meeting with the
mayor to discuss his investment in the Trinity River Project,
and a business lunch with one of his largest business
distributors. His afternoon was also full, but Pam would have
to clear it. He had more important business to attend to this
afternoon.

His right-hand man, Gordo, would arrange the rest of
his schedule so that he could resolve some of the more
annoying distractions with Victoria, Stefano and the meddling
law firm. They were all becoming loose ends that needed to be
wrapped up, and quickly. He would send Stefano out for his
final assignment and give him a chance to redeem himself.
And Victoria ... he smiled. He also had a plan for her. She
would contact Jeff one last time, and help put that particular
problem to rest.

Now that the bait was secured, his plan could move
along nicely. The first order of business was to make sure that
he was in a highly visible place – with a lot of witnesses. An
airtight alibi. The last thing he needed was another loose end;
there were already too many. Stefano was taking care of one of
them, if he could think with his head this time, but that was
only one.

He grunted disapprovingly as he thought about the mess at the diner the night before. He had come too far, and had too much riding on this, to let anyone screw it up. He had established himself in the community. He was trusted, respected and even honored. That diner incident wouldn't lead directly to him, obviously, but it was another mess to be handled, and got in the way of his ultimate goal.

When the time came for the next move, of course, Al would be sitting in a visible café, having a relaxed time and sipping a cup of coffee. First, though, he needed to assemble his organization for the final call with his team. They had rehearsed the plan and everyone was waiting for this moment. It was time.

Gordo had established simultaneous private line links to all key members of World One. Each member had their own connections to other members of the Senate, House, and essential White House staff... just plain old public information. The rest of the plan was a bit more complex. Private communications would be a real challenge. So Al had decided to get into the communications business. One of the companies he'd recently bought was a small telecom service company, who had just happened to sign agreements with all the national carriers. This company had been a reseller, but now began purchasing their own local lines, and providing their own service via satellite to the residents of Dallas.

Having this private link ensured that Al and his team could operate under the radar and away from prying ears. He could ensure that they would never be recorded by the government, and that they could operate in complete privacy. Protecting the identities of his team was imperative. Protecting the content of their discussions was absolutely necessary.

Each member had been provided with their own encrypted satellite service phone. Al spared no expense. With these private lines, he was able to reach his team without suspicion or fear of being caught. He looked out his office window now, and thought carefully about the plan. His team would help him be the man who sat in the Oval Office. This move was decades in the making, and he knew that he had the right team and the right contingencies in place to ensure success. The money couldn't be traced; it came from "anonymous" donations. And their shipments from Mexico would arrive in the morning, brilliantly hidden in two tons of woven fabric. It didn't hurt to have friends in customs.

His company had overseen many shipments from Mexico under the auspices of his NAFTA agreement for the textile business. He's had to make his fair share of sacrifices to get here, and agree to some pretty risky deals. Some people had died when they got too close, like that lawyer from Walker, Wright and Turner. He didn't think that it would lead back to him.

"Watch where you step." He laughed menacingly as he dramatized the fateful explosion himself. Then he grew serious. It shouldn't be a problem, really; by the time they got to the end of the trail, it would be too late.

Raul was in place, and waiting for the signal. All they had to do now was act.

He looked again at the list of members of World One. It took him a while to decode the garble. Each week was a new code. As he deciphered it, though, he saw that it was quite an impressive list, built over the past decade. They'd help him and his country, and they were all trained by the good old US of A. *Funny how things work out*, he thought.

He reached to the side of his desk and flipped the switch of the shredder, then took one last look at the list. He had been dreaming of this day, when he would have the world's most powerful country bowing to his influence, since he was young, and these were the people who were going to help him accomplish that goal. The list was an impressive array of high-ranking officials in all branches of the military, the Secret Service, the White House, and Congress. There were the police, of course, and even some employees of the post office. Most US entities had been infiltrated to some degree, and were now engaged with World One.

Grinning, he placed the paper in the shredder. The list went quickly through, and the shreds fell into the trashcan below.

He walked to the window in his office and watched as the cars arrived. He was looking forward to greeting Stan Flemming and speaking to the rest of the gentlemen from across the US – all part of this historic day. He thought about his father, and knew that he'd be proud of his only son. His father had hoped that Cuba would one day turn the tables on the United States of America and topple the greedy, power-mongering nation. Al was about to see that dream come true.

Gordo walked in, interrupting Al's thoughts. "We're ready for you."

Chapter 25

Kouros was the first to arrive at the scene. Lil came soon after him, and a barrage of police cars followed with sirens screaming, filling the streets from both directions. Kouros had his squad set a roadblock at the front of the neighborhood to check all vehicles leaving the area. When he reached Holly's house, he jumped out of his car and ran, pistol cocked, toward the open front door. Four other police personnel followed closely behind him. The chief stopped to the side of the front door, then thrust his gun through the open frame, pointing at its only target, Jeff Walker.

Jeff had fallen to his knees at the back of the living room, behind the couch.

He looked up at Kouros with a dazed expression "If I had gotten here sooner, if I'd come when she had asked me to .... we have to find her," he pleaded desperately.

Kouros surveyed the living room. "Don't touch anything," he said quietly. He turned to an officer on his right. "Get an investigator in here, now. And bring the camera." He knelt down by the first patch of blood on the carpet. "Have this analyzed. Jeff, do you know Holly's blood type?"

"Oh God," Jeff answered, burying his face in his hands.

When Lil walked in she let out an unplanned gasp. She spotted Jeff and ran to him before she realized what he was kneeling next to.

"Stop," Kouros demanded authoritatively.

Lil obeyed instantly, noting that she was inches away from a mass of a blood on the carpet. She began to see blackness, and fought for consciousness. Kouros came to her rescue, putting his arm around her for support and leading her to the couch.

The table was overturned next to the trail of blood. Clear red footprints led from the kitchen to the table, but from there the prints became thicker and looked more like streaks. An officer with a camera and notepad entered, asking everyone to clear the scene. Yellow crime scene tape began to enclose all the contents of Holly's living room.

Lil took a deep breath and looked at Jeff. She took a few feeble steps around the couch and slumped down next to him. They locked into each other's arms, shocked.

"Check the back yard. We've got a window broken here, appears to be some blood," an officer recited methodically to another officer and a small recording device. "We've got two officers, DOA. Need further information from an autopsy to determine actual cause of death." The officer walked the room from the front door to the back window, and back to the front.

"We've got footprints back here!" an officer yelled from the kitchen

Lil shut the officers out, trying desperately to think of the words to say to Jeff. Her mind raced faster than her mouth could even move, though she felt paralyzed and her body felt numb. The contradiction in what her mind and body experiencedleft her feeling nearly helpless. Her heart, though, ached with overwhelming loss. Jeff had known Holly for years, and she'd become a good friend to the entire firm. To think that she was gone, or at least missing...

Her hands shook as she tried to steady herself and help Jeff to his feet.

"Jeff, I have to talk to you," she finally managed. She spoke very carefully, wondering if he had the strength to hear her right now. "The police say that we may be in danger too. We have to leave town." Jeff listened closely, but shook his head.

"We have to find Holly, Lil. I'm not going anywhere until I find her."

Lil shook her head firmly. "No. The police will do all they can. We can't do any more, but they'll keep us informed. We can't just be sitting ducks. You don't know who we're dealing with here." She paused and took a deep breath, thinking carefully about her next words. "Bob sent me something, his last day at the office. It's probably what got him killed."

Jeff finally looked up to focus directly on Lil. "What do you mean? Bob sent you something?"

Lil nodded again, looking down. "It's a membership list, Jeff. It's a World One membership list." They finally reached the street, ushered by the police, and found their way past the yellow tape marking off the parked police car.

Jeff avoided looking at the sheet-covered figures in the car, and stared instead at Lil. "What?" he asked, surprised.

"Bob had somehow uncovered a secret list. And it's not Stan Flemming who's running the show. Bob started tracking a paper trail on the money being donated by World One. This money wasn't ending up in the hands of children, Jeff. Anonymous donations were being made to the committee to re-elect the president. Money was being distributed to each member of World One, and those members span across all of our government agencies. But it doesn't stop there. Apparently, instead of reporting this as income to the committee fund, it was marked returned. It became untraceable at that point. Bob believed it was ending up in the pockets of someone at the White House, in addition to people in the government agencies that received these funds. There were guys; names on this list, Jeff. Guys we know and trusted." Lil frowned in concentration, her head clearing as she became more involved in her story.

"Bob was getting close to uncovering something big. He told an FBI agent what he had found. That's when he started getting those phone calls. And he sent me the e-mail the night he was killed. The agent had told him not to tell us about it, because we might muddy the waters. He'd finally decided that the agent was double crossing him, and that he should tell us after all."

She looked down, and Jeff was silent. His mind raced as he began putting the pieces together. Al was buying favor with people in very high places. This was how they got to Kevin. This was how they had such good coverage. What were these men getting in return? A promise of a role in the next government? One thing was for sure: No one was to be trusted.

Chapter 26

Gordo sat quietly in his chair in the room located deep under the ground of the Al Chord's estate. He'd arranged the call and all the players were in position. And this was the perfect place for such a meeting. White unmarked vans had started arriving at the Chord estate two years ago, under the guise of new landscaping and groundwork, with workers in unmarked, bland uniforms. For two years, bands of white vans had come and gone. The men from these vans worked secretly, excavating what would become World Two – the quiet headquarters of Al Chord's plan. Outfitted with the latest telecom equipment, satellite feeds, and computers, the rooms were fully operational and ready for action. Today was the culmination of that plan. Gordo looked around now, taking in the massive underground bunker secretly tucked away under the estate, and realized that the time had come.

***

Al had assembled over 6,500 key operatives around the country. Each was now waiting for his or her final instructions. He walked slowly but purposely down the wide hallway of his house, and stopped at an unmarked door. Opening the door revealed a small closet, with various coats hanging on the small rack, and boxes up on the shelf above his head. He reached behind the last coat on his right and found the switch. It had been carefully designed, and could easily pass for a light switch if you didn't know what you were looking for. He flicked it for perhaps the last time now, and the room morphed into a door, the rack, boxes, and wall at the back sliding to the right to reveal a long hallway.

He walked in, feeling the cool air wafting up from below. The floor became a grate, and he could hear computers whirring below. At the end of the hallway was another door, which was attached to a motion sensor. The top of the door slid into the ceiling, revealing a camera. This piece of equipment took a quick snapshot of Al's eyes, ran its program, and recognized him as a valid participant. The entire door and camera now lifted into the ceiling, revealing a small elevator. He stepped in and sped down, two stories below the Chord estate, to the World Two bunker.

His estate was quite large and built to accept discerning guests. There were several entrances around the grounds, and the ones used today would provide the most privacy and security. At the opposite end of the 5-acre estate was a discreet loading dock and landscape entrance. Some of the guests knew to enter from this area, where they followed the same procedure, with a quick eye scan and recognition program. Gordo and Al greeted each guest as they arrived. From the entrance, the guests were taken through the long tunnels and secret elevator back to the meeting room.

Al's anticipation of this moment increased with each step toward the conference room, where thousands of loyal compadres awaited his words. He had people there in person, as well as people on the phone and through computer connections. Stan Flemming was waiting patiently, seated at the back of the room. Gordo walked around Al and joined Stan at the table, waiting for Al to enter. Al had been working since he was eighteen years old, when he moved from Cuba to Mexico, and then ultimately to the United States, to build a network that would give him the power and influence to pull this off. He had met with many leaders under the cloak of darkness and discretion, money and promise of power in hand, to personally recruit all 6,500 of the men in his organization.

It had been painstaking and tedious, and he had done it with the passion and precision of a surgeon. It had taken nearly thirty years of his life to get to this point, and many members of his extended family in Cuba had dedicated more years to this cause.

He took his seat and reached for the blinking red button of the conference phone. He hadn't written a speech, but had rehearsed these lines for the last thirty years, and knew exactly what he wanted to say.

"Welcome, gentlemen," he said warmly. "We have arrived at a time when opportunity abounds. Our plans have already borne fruit, and moved us toward the freedom of our new America." He looked at Gordo and pointed toward the seat across from him, indicating that Gordo should take his seat.

"Stan Flemming has courageously led a pre-emptive campaign in both the government and the media. Without him, we could not have held our meetings and made our plans, or maintained our anonymity. And I'd like to thank my trusted advisor and confidant, Gordon Lipscomb. Without *him*, we would not have the brilliant tactical plan in place to make our dreams a reality. Pure brilliance. World One will soon lead the country to its rightful destiny. The arrogance of its current government will be no more. Each one of you plays a part in making this happen. You should each have received a coded plan document from my office yesterday. Gordo will announce the decoder sequence at the end of this call. At that time, you are to review the plans closely and then destroy them. At noon today, you should all should take your places, and at 1 p.m. we will make history.

"This is a turning point, people. One we should all be proud to be part of. You will hear from me again, from our new command post in Washington, DC. Thank you and God speed to each of you."

He stood slowly and handed the call over to Gordo, who would close with the pertinent details. Within minutes, Gordo clicked the button in satisfaction. No one would stop them now.

"Gentleman," Al said, dismissing the men around the table. He shook their hands as they were guided outside of the room. After the last man left, he turned to Gordo.

"Gordo, the shipment came in two days ago. Did you get the goods distributed to all the major checkpoints?" he asked out of habit.

"You know I did. All parties confirmed this morning that they received their packages. Each sub-command post distributed their lot last night to lower the risk of detection, just as planned. So far, no local authorities have been tipped off about our activities. Our friendly officers down there have kept us very informed."

"Well, they will all know our plans soon enough."

Chapter 27

Jeff and Lil settled into a cold, stale, and barren room at the back of the station. Both huddled around a steaming cup of coffee, and both stared at the floor, uncommunicative. As soon as the door closed behind the two officers, Jeff turned to Lil.

"Lil, we have to find Holly," he said again.

She shook her head. "Jeff, I have the list of the World One members here." She shuffled through her purse, pulling out a rather inconspicuous piece of paper. "See for yourself. I'm sure that these guys are behind Holly's abduction. They aren't playing around. If we can find them, we may be able to figure out where she is, and who has her." She watched Jeff scan the list of names.

He gasped in disbelief as his eyes ran down the list. "Shit."

Lil nodded again, confirming his statement. "We have to let the police do their jobs. And this will probably pull in the FBI. But look at the names on that list – a lot of them *are* police. And it's not only police and government officials. If they're into what Bob thought they were into, that means that some of the most successful business people in the country are crooked–"

Before she could finish, Kouros entered the room with two of his young officers. Another officer stood watch outside of the room.

"I've found something that I think you guys need to see," he told them, looking from Jeff to Lil, and back again. "We sent some officers to your office to look for any pertinent information, particularly in Bob's files. Among the hundreds of cases he's handled this year, we found one that seemed rather odd." He handed a file over to Jeff and Lil. Jeff grabbed it and flipped it open before Lil could even hold out her hand.

"Someone beat us to your office, though. The place was a wreck. Made to look like a robbery, but given everything I think that's not the likely MO. In spite of the mess, the case files seemed to be intact. And we found this."

"What is this? It's empty." Jeff closed the file and looked for a file name. "U.S. Industries vs. International Exchange Co. I remember this case, but not well. Bob handled it; he felt like it was an open-and-shut case. Something about a trade dispute. So?" He handed the file back impatiently.

Kouros shrugged. "All of the other files were filled to capacity and filed by date. This file was in the most recent months. And it was the only file that had no notes, no file information. It didn't make sense. So I had one of our guys look it up at the court." He paused for effect. "Apparently it was a trade dispute over a US company who felt that NAFTA was allowing International Exchange Company to move into its markets with below-market prices, designed to put them out of business."

Jeff and Lil still stared blankly at Kouros. They didn't see the relevance, and were both becoming impatient.

"Do you know who owns International Exchange Company?" Kouros handed another paper to Lil. "Al Chord. Name sounded familiar, so we did some more checking. Bob Wright apparently became suspicious of Al Chord's shipping practices after this case, and demanded an audit of their shipments. The court agreed, and the audit was scheduled for this week."

Lil frowned. "I still don't get what this has to do with Holly or Bob. Are you saying Al Chord had something to do with Bob's death? I don't see the connection."

"Well, Chord wasn't exactly thrilled about this audit. We checked phone records and found that some calls were placed to Bob Wright directly from International Exchange Company. One call was placed the day before Bob was killed." Kouros took a deep breath. "The pieces aren't all together yet, but we feel like there's enough information here to investigate Al Chord. This is a major businessman – very powerful – and Bob had crossed him. They had ongoing communications, up until Bob was murdered. It's fishy. The FBI is also involved. We've got everyone on this." He tried to muster a smile, but he was getting weary from the long hours, and was old enough to feel it. "I'm getting too old for this," he noted, grinning wryly at the lawyers.

"But how do we know who to trust?" Lil blurted out.

"He's ok, Lil, show him the list," Jeff answered.

Lil handed Kouros the list of World One members and the room fell silent while he read through it. He began to frown.

"Interesting list." He turned back to the file, and looked again at Lil and Jeff. "I suspected this was happening," Kouros added. "But it was hard to prove. So you're suggesting that this list is a list of bought-and-paid-for men now working directly for Al?"

"We don't know, but there seems to be a connection," Jeff responded dryly.

"Interesting."

"And that list has gotten several people dead, Kouros," Jeff added. "Bob didn't stand a chance. He was the one who forwarded the list, which means he was working on this as well as Chord's textile company. He had two counts against him, as far as Chord was concerned."

"So we need to deal with that. I have a couple of guys on the team that are my neighbors. We play poker together, and I know that they're on the up and up. I'll ask them to scout out some of the guys on this list. In the meantime, consider what I've just told you. Try to think of any other connections. Brian here is going to ask a few more questions regarding this new information, to see what we can figure out. Please share everything you know."

He turned toward the door, then turned back. "We'll be moving you to a safe house that the FBI often uses in drug cases. You'll both be safe there until we can find something more permanent."

"One more thing," Jeff muttered quickly. "I got a visit last night from two people claiming to work with Al Chord. They said that we're in grave danger. Said that there's a master plan here. Said they'd send someone to help. At this point I don't know who to trust or what to believe. We should all watch our backs."

His mind reeled with the information and the thought of Holly and, without any other alternative, he closed his eyes and asked God to look after her. *Keep her until I find her, God help her. God help us all.*

***

Victoria stared at the phone for what seemed to be an eternity, then finally grabbed the receiver, holding the crumpled piece of paper in her left hand. She didn't need the paper anymore; she'd committed the number to memory after the tenth attempt to call. Still, it was something to squeeze while she waited.

A voice answered, and her mind raced. She waited for the repetition of the greeting, then sighed and dove in.

"Jeff, this is Victoria from the Brooklyn." She heard herself saying the words, as though she was listening from a distance. This was possibly the most dangerous call she'd ever made, and it felt that way. "I have more information for you ... information about Holly."

Silence reigned on the other end of the line, and she wondered if she'd lost him.

***

"How did you know how to reach me? And what do you know about Holly?" Jeff asked loudly. He waved at Lil to come closer. They were in the safe house, and alone in the room, though he knew that there were undercover cops downstairs. They had insisted that it was safe, and completely unknown. That didn't explain how Victoria had found him here.

"You have some nerve!" he continued, his mind racing. "You show up at my house and while you're there, something happens to my friend. Who are you, and what do you want from me? What do you know about all of this? Did you have anything to do with Holly's disappearance?"

"Jeff, she's my friend too, and I want her safe. Just listen. I'm trying to help. You don't know who you're dealing with. You're not safe, and you won't be safe, no matter where you go. They have eyes everywhere. I can't talk here. We need to meet," she said firmly. "Never mind how I found you. If I found you, it means that they can find you too, and that should make you very worried."

"What's going on here, Victoria? How do you know so much? And how are you working with Stan? No one knows about Holly, not even the media. How did you know..." He was getting irritated with Victoria's vague responses. He'd been told that the phone line was secure, and that only the police had the unlisted number. They were under strict instructions not to place any calls without notifying the police stationed outside first, to ensure that they were untraced. The fact that Victoria had rung through worried him, as did her statement about anyone else finding the house.

"I told you that I can't talk right now. We must meet. Meet me at the diner at 11 this morning. That's two hours from now. You must come alone. And tell no one that you have spoken with me. I'm risking everything by calling you. You must trust me."

***

Victoria didn't let Jeff finish his questions. She slid the phone into its cradle after the last word, disconnecting the line, and looked down at her hands. When she finally looked up, Al was staring at her. She tried to avoid eye contact with him.

"Good job, Victoria. We can't afford any loose ends, remember." He stood up from the couch, which ran the length of one of the walls in his second living area and walked slowly toward her to place his hand on her shoulder. Then he grabbed the phone and dialed another number.

"Gordo, everything's in motion. Get everyone in place." He hung up the phone, gave Victoria's shoulder another quick squeeze, and left the room.

Chapter 28

"It's your move, *compadre*." Al spoke deliberately into the secured phone line, his mouth a grim line. "No games. This is what we have worked all of our lives for. At noon today, exactly two hours from now, all troops will take their places across the country to secure the local authorities. We have a counterattack unit surrounding DC. The ground unit will move in at 12:30 p.m. precisely. They should have all primary targets secured at 12:45 p.m. You should have your target fixed at 1 p.m. Do not make any moves, however, until you hear from me. If something should happen to me, you will follow procedures as outlined in our counterattack document. Understood?"

His anticipation was growing every moment, and he took a deep breath to slow his heart rate. It was important to maintain his cool on the outside. He was on the brink of a historic event.

"No problem, my friend. We have gone over this many times. Your country is proud, and we'll stand with you and our allies upon your success." The voice on the other line was thick and raspy, but the message was clear. Cuba would reign and the world would watch.

"Your father is proud to look down on you. Now Cuba can truly be free from the influence and judgment of an unholy government. Our flag will fly proudly, and those of you in the

United States can stand with us for a new day of opportunity," the man continued.

Al listened as his uncle spoke with great passion, and heard the emotions in his voice. Pablo was Al's father's only brother, and had stood with Al throughout the decades to help seize victory this final day.

He reflected on his past and the economic and political environment that had helped his cause. He knew that the American summit, from which Cuba was excluded, had only added to his cause. Cuba's crime was simply to fight for its freedom, its solidarity, and its beliefs, but the U.S. saw it as much more. The economic sanctions that the U.S. had leveled against Cuba in response had opposition, though, and that opposition generally consisted of Al's team. Many others in the U.S. also disagreed with the president's position and the five-decades-old economic sanctions. The fight for democracy and capitalism left Cuba and others wondering if perhaps there was a better way.

Al knew that there was, and the United States would be liberated with it.

He closed the conversation and quickly gathered all the sensitive information, shredding every piece of paper he could find and searching his desk for any missed items. He absolutely couldn't leave anything behind; nothing could lead the authorities back to him. At 1 p.m. today, Al Chord would cease to exist. At 1 p.m., Alfonso de Cordova would once again emerge, victorious.

He wished more of his family were alive to watch his country's success. The wealth and power he would bring to his people would be insurmountable. The U.S. government would no longer be in a feeding frenzy, devouring smaller countries and weaker peoples. It would no longer push its capitalistic values on nations not interested in adopting this self-indulging way. His group of friends and supporters reached far and wide, and they were about to offer him a one-way invitation to the White House.

Al walked by the living area, where the door was still open. He could see Victoria's silhouette, still seated on the brown leather couch. Her face was in her hands and she was sobbing. But she'd chosen to join him, he reminded himself. She had made this bargain, and now she had to follow through.

"Victoria, it's time," he said, pausing in the doorway. "This is no time to grow a conscience. Put this behind you, and I'll allow you to live in my country with no hassles. Think of the alternative. You know me too well to try to cross me." He walked decidedly over to her and grabbed one of her hands.

***

She resolved to do what he asked and did not resist as he lifted her to her feet.

"You'll be fine."

He did not step back, but pulled her closer to him and caressed her tear-streaked face. She felt his warm breath on her face and looked fearlessly into his dark eyes, defying him to break her spirit. His chiseled features and deep olive skin made him close to irresistible. Both of them stood defiant to any threat the other tried to use, and she sighed. She had fallen into his arms so easily, so many times before, when she sought to forget the rest of the world. She knew that her desire for him overtook her reason. Now the thought of Jeff lingered in her mind, and she found strength knowing that for once she would make the right decision, no matter the cost.

***

Al always separated business from pleasure, but with Victoria he could feel the lines blurring, and he yearned for her voluptuous body. The light behind him made her dress almost transparent, and it was more than he could resist. His mind raced as his eyes traveled along her curves, which spelled perfection. His desire was overcoming his control.

They stood quietly, each looking for any sign of weakness in the other. He slid his hand from her cheek to follow her strong jaw, then brushed it through the silken hair at the nape of her neck. He grabbed her there and pulled her closer to his warm body. Her face relaxed, and her mouth fell slightly open. She was following his every move.

Al closed his eyes and regained his control. He recited his plan over in his head and refused to let a woman take his mind away from his mission.

"Victoria. At 11 a.m. you will do what you need to do. Then I will protect you." He smiled at her in a way that melted most women, his dark, straight hair glistening from the light at the opposite end of the room.

Victoria's guard immediately took over, and she stood strongly against any new advances he might try to make. Her jaw tightened.

He stepped away from her and dismissed the woman with a wave of his hand, then walked out the door and toward his next appointment.

Chapter 29

Gordo pulled slowly up to the warehouse, and paused to watch the cranes lifting their precious cargo from the ship. He hated Houston, but this was a special occasion. This cargo was instrumental to Al's plan, and he would personally ensure that it was delivered without mistakes. Each dockworker was on his payroll, and he knew that everything would go smoothly; he had spent the better part of the last year developing relationships with them, and knew about their lives. He knew their kids' names, who their wives were, and even whether they had mistresses. He knew their birthdays and their favorite beers. Gordo had done his homework and he would take care of it all. He took personal accountability for the success of Al's plan. He had flown into Houston that morning, and driven over to the ship yard to see that the shipment had arrived and made it into the right hands.

Satisfied that it had, he got out of his truck and walked up to the unloading and loading dock.

"Carlos!" he exclaimed as he met the first man walking toward the ship. "How're the kids? What are they, five and nine now? Got your hands full, my friend." Gordo shot the man his best buddy smile and shook his hand vigorously.

"Gordo! Came to personally see this one in, eh?" Carlos waddled over to the dock. With every step, he had to work hard to swing his 250-pound, 6-foot frame. His meaty legs struggled to get past each other with each thrust forward, and Gordo shook his head in disgust. That was no way to live, but it also wasn't his problem.

"We've got ten pallets unloaded already. They're over there." Carlos pointed to the side of the warehouse. "We've still got ten more to unload. This load is pretty heavy, buddy. What do you have in these cartons?" Carlos usually didn't ask any questions, but his curiosity was getting the best of him this time.

"You ask too many questions, my friend." Gordo slipped another wad of money into the man's still-open hand, quickly dampening any curiosity Carlos had about the mysterious load, and ensuring silence from that point forward.

"I'd say you have a lot of pretty damn heavy blankets here," Carlos laughed heartily.

"It's the good weave down in Mexico," Gordo agreed dryly. He walked purposely toward the shift manager, who sat in the small station house at the front of the warehouse.

The man saw him approaching and stood from his place behind the desk. "Gordo, I got your message and checked the load myself. It's all accounted for. We're about halfway there. It'll be unloaded by about 7 this morning." JJ checked his watch and then reached for a Styrofoam cup. The steam rose slowly, and Gordo could smell the waft of warm, rich coffee.

JJ saw him staring and smiled. "Go ahead, help yourself. The coffee's in the front office. The trucks are running behind schedule, but they'll be here to pick up your load by about 7:30. Yep, about thirty minutes after we unload the last pallet. Shit, can't these guys stay on time? I got a dock to run."

He looked haggard this morning, Gordo thought. Must have been a late night last night. His wife, Ginger, must have kept him busy. Gordo's face glazed over as his mind wandered to the possibilities there, but JJ interrupted his thoughts.

"Gotta run down to see how the boys are doin'," he said. "Make yourself at home." He grabbed his clipboard and started toward the ship.

Gordo spotted another dockworker around the unloaded pallets, and headed toward him as JJ left.

"Hey man," Gordo shouted, "I need to move one of these pallets into the warehouse, to do a spot check on the contents. Can you help me with that?" This was a pretty regular request by auditors, so the worker didn't think twice about it.

"Anything for you, man," he agreed. "And thanks for the case of Shiner. You got good taste. Nothin' like it." The man slapped Gordo on the back as he headed for the forklift on the other side of the palettes.

Gordo found the front office while he waited to get his pallet in the warehouse. He spotted the coffee and poured himself a large, steaming cup. It was an early morning for him, too, and he hadn't been by the coffee shop on his way here. He dumped in a little sugar and a little cream, and was on his way. The window in the office gave him a great view of the forklift, and he saw that the man had already moved the pallet into the warehouse. Instinctively, the worker started to open one of the boxes to make it easier for Gordo to "audit."

Gordo ran out of the office, spilling half of the hot coffee on his pants. "Hey, don't touch that!" he shouted.

The man spun around, surprised. "Jesus, man. Just trying to help out."

Gordo realized that hot coffee was running down his leg, and that he'd been hasty in his reaction. "Shit!" he said, clenching his teeth against the burn. "God, that hurts."

He opened his eyes and waved to the worker with his free hand. "Sorry, man. Just a little jittery this morning. Probably too much coffee." He tried to muster a laugh, though when it finally came out, it was more than a little forced. "It's my ass if anything happens to this shipment. We've got a pretty tight-ass customer up in Dallas and he's got us running around like a bunch of shits. Sorry, man. Thanks for the help." He extended his hand to the man, who still stood frozen in shock.

Slowly, the other man extended his hand. "Jesus, don't do that. You scared the shit out of me. I thought the goddamn thing was going to explode by the way you yelled out." The man shook his head and headed back to work on the dock.

Gordo grimaced again, still trying to ignore the pain of his scorched legs. He threw the cup at the garbage can about 5 feet away, disgusted with himself. It would have been his ass if that man had looked inside the boxes. It might still be his ass if someone told Al that he'd made such a scene.

But as long as he was here, he needed to make sure that the shipments were secure, and that they contained what they were supposed to. He took his pocketknife out and carefully opened the first box on the pallet. The top layer was colorful, woven fabric, as promised, but he kept digging until he found what he was looking for. About halfway down the box, he touched the cold metal object. He felt for the handle and used all his strength to pull the case toward the top of the box.

Checking around to make sure that there was no one watching, he pulled the case out and opened it up. The array of weapons in front of him was quite impressive. Black, shiny AK45 rifles and self-activating hand-launch missiles, to name just a few. And each box had its own stock of new weapons. Gordo closed the case and quickly put it back in its original resting place in the box. He heaved the top back on and settled it into place.

Five minutes later, he was back in his Durango, headed back toward Dallas. Shipment confirmed and ready.

Chapter 30

**Four months earlier, at the case of US Industries vs.
International Trade Corp.**

"Your honor, this case is cut and dried." Bob Wright
adjusted his tie before he stood to address the court.

"International Exchange is deliberately lowering their
prices to drive out local competition. This is not in the spirit of
the NAFTA agreement, and I will show the court the specific
ways in which U.S. laws on fair competition are being broken."
Bob enjoyed litigation. He certainly didn't back down from a
fight, regardless of how powerful the company on the opposing
side was.

"I maintain that in order to understand the full extent
of this blatant shunning of U.S. laws, we must be able to
examine the ways in which International Exchange delivers its
products to the market. They maintain that their processes
allow them to offer such affordable prices. But my client
maintains that manufacturing processes, even with cheaper
labor, cannot account for the price difference this company has
introduced into their competing markets." He handed a file to
the judge.

"I am requesting an audit of the records of Al Chord
and International Exchange. This will put an end to any
speculation as to the means of offering such prices. I expect
that IEC will want to make public their claims, to end these

speculations and go forward with their business." He strode confidently to his seat.

"I object, your honor." IEC's lawyer stood defiantly. "Mr. Wright here is asking us to pull thousands of documents to prove what point? He is merely stalling because he has no other evidence of any wrongdoing." The young woman continued to stand, looking defiantly at Bob.

The judge pursed his lips. "I will allow it, Ms. Gray. There is just cause to pull these records. Your client must submit these documents to the court by close of business Monday. We will reconvene on Wednesday, after both parties have reviewed them."

The woman grunted in disappointment and sat, defeated.

"The court is now in recess, we will adjourn here on Wednesday at 8 a.m."

Bob collected his papers and caught a glance of Al Chord at the other table. If looks could kill, Bob knew he'd be a dead man. He'd seen it before, though, and he just stared back.

The young woman caught the exchanged looks and quickly advised her client to maintain control.

Bob decided then that he wanted to find out more about Al Chord. He was surprised that the man had shown up personally for this case, and was equally surprised that he showed so much emotion about an audit. Sure, pulling records wasn't fun, but someone else was going to have to do the legwork there, and this disclosure seemed to particularly disturb Al Chord. What exactly were in those documents that he didn't want seen?

Bob realized immediately that Al's attorneys would stall on the disclosure and present a case for more time. He suspected that they might see those documents within months, if they were lucky. It was more likely that they would ask for years. He also suspected that there might be a case of "lost" documents. *Lost to shredding*, he amended quietly. Either way, he'd got a read on Al, and his read was that the man was not to be trusted.

He nodded to himself, then jotted down a note on his pad – *Connection to World One?* His instincts told him that there was definitely a connection, and he needed to find out how. He'd seen shell companies used many times in the past, and what he'd uncovered so far, while so far very loosely connected, all seemed to lead him back to Al Chord.

One way or another, he was going to get to the bottom of what the two meant to each other.

Chapter 31

Jeff grabbed a seat near the back of the diner and turned so that he could see the front door. The waiter took his drink order, and he settled in for the wait. He was fifteen minutes early, and this was intentional – he wanted to see who came and went, and watch for any setups. He didn't trust the woman, or the situation, and had walked the entire diner before he found a seat with a good view of the door, watching the faces of everyone in the diner, looking for anyone familiar or suspicious. There were approximately fifteen undercover officers roaming the street outside, working at the restaurant, and eating at the restaurant. Or so he'd been told. He didn't know any of them, so he looked at each person within eyesight to try to figure out who was a cop and who was not.

If he could spot the cops, he knew it would be trouble – anyone used to looking for them would see them in a heartbeat, and that could mean his life.

He grabbed the beer out of the waiter's hand when he brought it, and gulped half of it down without thinking, then set it on the table and stared at it for what seemed like forever. This situation made him incredibly nervous, and he wasn't dealing with it well.

"Jeff?"

The sweet voice forced him out of his blank stare and he looked up and quickly stood, nearly knocking over the table. "Victoria."

The blonde was standing in front of him, as beautiful as ever, though she looked very tired. He waited for her to sit on the other side of the table, then took his seat again.

"Seeing you twice in one day. Why? And what do you know about Holly?" he demanded suddenly. There was no point in beating around the bush; he wanted to get this over and done as quickly as possible.

Victoria didn't waste any time either. She didn't want to be here, and she certainly didn't want to be doing this. She avoided eye contact, looking down at the table and playing with her long fingernails, but answered immediately. "Jeff, I know that Holly was kidnapped. She's still alive, but you must do as I say or you will never see her again."

His mouth fell open as he searched for a response. Finally he found his voice. "How do you know this?"

"I have contacts, as you know, and they're reliable. I've already told you that I'm working with Al Chord's group. I didn't know that he meant to kidnap Holly, or I would have warned you. As soon as I heard, I wanted to help." She let her eyes search the table in front of her, afraid to see the desperation on his face.

His suspicions rose as he listened to her speak. She was right – she was working with this group, and they'd now kidnapped his best friend. She might say that she wanted to help, but she was a part of the group that had put Holly in danger, and he wasn't inclined to trust her. "How are you working with Al and Stan? And did they have anything to do with this? How are you involved? What do they want with Holly?" He rattled off the questions as they came to him, without waiting for any responses.

She shook her head, indicating that she was unable to answer most of them. "You must leave the city. And you must separate yourself from your law firm. Stop digging into other people's affairs. It will get you killed, and it will spell Holly's death. I took a great risk coming to see you, and I'm afraid that may have hurt Holly."

Jeff stared at the beautiful woman, shocked, and realized that Holly wasn't the only one in danger here. This beautiful girl in front of him had been pulled into the dark side as well, and her life might be in danger. His heart welled in his chest as he thought about what could happen to her too.

He grabbed her hands, squeezing them and looking directly into her face. "Look at me, Victoria. You must look at me. The moment I saw you, you captured my attention and I wanted to know more about you. I can't explain it. If you're involved in something, you must tell me. We can help each other. Don't do this. Why were you at Bob's that day?"

"I can't," she managed to say, seemingly stifling her emotions. "You have to leave, Jeff. It's too late for me, but you can get away. You must save yourself. I tried to get out, but they want me to stay in. I'm the only one that has gotten close, and pulling me out now would compromise the mission. I know what's in store for me. But for you, there's still time."

She pulled away from him and tried to rise from the booth, but he reached toward her and grabbed her arm.

"Jeff, you aren't safe," she pled. "Al is already on his way to DC. It's too late for me, so I have nothing to lose. And there are some things you need to know." She spoke in a whisper, her voice rushed and tense with the secrets she was about to reveal. "Al is planning something terrible. You must try to stop him. If you don't, he'll kill you, and many other people."

Jeff's mind reeled. "What is he planning? You keep telling me he's planning something terrible, but if I don't know what it is then I can't help. You have to give me more information."

As Jeff was asking the question, though, he noticed four men rushing toward him. They reached Victoria, who was still sitting at the table, and one of them grabbed her. It took only seconds for Jeff to register that the other three were after him. He looked around to find the officers who were there to protect him, but no one in the restaurant was moving. They were either already gone, or being paid to look the other way, he realized. He was on his own. He turned around to find an exit.

He heard a shot behind him, and looked over his should to see Victoria hanging by her arms, blood streaming down her face.

"No!" he shouted. He struggled with his conscience, but saw the gun pointed straight at him, and knew where the next bullet was going to land.

He turned and ran like hell.

The kitchen was behind them, and he ran as fast as he could toward the swinging door. His baseball skills began to show as he skillfully and quickly sidestepped the waiters, missing all obstacles between him and safety. The kitchen was long, but he could see a door to the outside world toward the end of the hallway area. He could also hear loud voices behind him, accompanied by falling dishes, shouts, and rattling pans. They were close, but he didn't look back.

His car was parked in the lot next to the restaurant, so he ran full speed in that direction, still stepping around surprised restaurant staff.

With his last few steps, he fluidly reached for the keys in his jacket pocket. With one click, the car was open and ready to go. Jeff ran across the lot and jumped in the car pressing the start button to bring the Porsche to life, pausing to look toward the restaurant and try to memorize the faces of the three men running for him. After a moment of looking, though, he realized that they were going to get too close before he memorized anything.

He jammed the car into gear, turned toward them, and jumped on the gas. The men instinctively rolled to the side, missing his car by inches as he roared by.

His heart raced as he guided the Porsche quickly through the side streets, and his mind burned with questions. Where were the officers who were supposed to be in the restaurant? Why Victoria? What did she have to do with this? And why Holly? Were they specifically going after the important women in his life? The pieces were there, but he couldn't make them fit. He pointed his car for the safe house, intent on finding Lil.

Right now he didn't know who he could trust, but he didn't think either of them was safe.

He reached for his phone and scrolled for her cell number. He had insisted that she keep the phone with her at all times, in case he needed to reach her.

She answered immediately, and he gave her the abbreviated version of the story. "Meet me at the park near Main and Third," he huffed, still out of breath from the run to the car.

She agreed, then continued, "Jeff, I don't know what's going on, but the officers here are frantic. It's going to be hard to get out of here unnoticed. They're covering every door of this place, and they won't let me out of their sight. They must know about what happened at the restaurant."

"Lil, I don't know if they can be trusted. There weren't any officers in the restaurant. Unless those were officers…" He paused, his mind running through the possibilities. Quite a few officers were on Al Chord's payroll, and he wondered now how many were still on the force … and supposedly guarding them. "We need to get out of here. I don't know where…" His voice trailed off again. "But I'll think of something."

He thought about the World One list and wondered if Kouros had been able to eliminate any of the threats from his own force on that list. He had to, or they'd end up falling victim to them, thinking they were friends. He hoped the former was true and that there were fewer threats from fewer people for he and Lil to deal with.

"Give me twenty minutes," Lil said quickly. "I'll create some sort of distraction to get out of here."

"Hang on to your phone. It's our lifeline now. Call me if you have any problems."

Chapter 32

Alfonso de Cordova thought about what he would say to his people when this was all over. The troops were in place and securing their targets right now, and he could taste the victory. Looking out the window of his limo, he could see the White House in plain view. It brought a sly smile to his face.

He had taken his private jet from Addison Airport straight to Dulles, where his private car service awaited. For the next hour he would sit at a café across the street from the White House, waiting for the troops he had stationed in DC. Everyone knew their part, and he was confident it would be flawlessly executed. He'd thought of everything, and if he hadn't thought of it, he'd paid someone else to do so.

His comrades south of the border were preparing their missiles for their U.S. targets now. Yes, the U.S. military intelligence would notice, but by then it would be too late. He glanced at his watch again; the teams whose primary targets covered the major media cities would have them secure within the next five minutes. He would control what the people heard, through these media outlets, and keep the nation from panicking. His national broadcast would happen soon enough.

He spotted the cafe and pointed it out to his driver. Gordo should be there already, to confirm that all was being executed to plan.

His driver, another member of World One, would wait at the back of the cafe for his signal.

His phone rang unexpectedly, and he picked it up. He frowned as he listened to the voice on the other end; they had lost Jeff, the man said, but they would find him. Many of the officers in Dallas were on his payroll, and they were coming in handy now. They would be most helpful in tracking this man down, and were already securing the airports.

Al clenched his hands and took a deep breath. Victoria hadn't managed Jeff Walker as she was supposed to, and it looked like she might have screwed up the meeting on purpose. He straightened his tie; he'd wondered if she would stick to the plan, or if she would try to play the hero. It looked now as if she had chosen the latter.

He paused for a moment, thinking about her, then spoke the words. "Kill her," he told the man. "Just kill her."

He hung up the phone and stepped out of the limo into the crisp spring air, taking a deep breath and trying to remember all the details of this day. As he waved off his driver, a small crowd of tourists walking toward the cafe stopped to watch and see if the person getting out of the limo was some type of celebrity. He waved cheerily at them. This was the day he'd been living for, and he was feeling magnanimous.

He also knew that he looked like royalty, with his dark European shades, dark, straight hair, and deep bronze skin. He smiled at the crowd and walked toward the café, striding forward with purpose. No one stopped him or argued with him; his power was obvious, and somewhat frightening.

When he got to the café, he took a seat near the front, where he would have a good view of the White House. He looked at it with pride and ordered a cup of coffee, then settled in patiently for the wait.

***

"Move it, move it, move it!" Lieutenant Smith yelled to his troops. Each team member had a security badge, provided compliments of insiders for World One. They were getting into the most secure areas with no problem. Their weapons were strapped to their legs and bodies, hidden from sight, and they had their orders.

As soon as they reached the secured area where they knew the members of cabinet were scheduled to be, they unstrapped their weapons and began securing the location.

Staffers on the other end of the hall heard the shots ringing through the halls of the White House and ran at the sound, ducking under tables and diving into open doors. Everyone panicked and scrambled to move away from the shots.

"Watch your back! Move to the front!" Lieutenant Smith's voice continued to command his troops. He looked at his watch. Three minutes left.

The first team of four reached the Secretary of State. Their orders were to restrain their targets and place them in a secured area, but keep them alive. The second team found the Oval Office and secured all the doors. This would be their holding area.

"Cover me!" one team member yelled as he moved to the second hallway. The White House security team moved in, shooting at the invaders. They came late, but brought greater numbers than the Lieutenant's group had.

"Shoot to kill!" a member of the White House team yelled.

One invading team member went down with the first volley of shots. The rest of the team stepped over his body and walked toward the White House security team, shooting. Two bullets found their targets, and two men went down. The lieutenant jumped into the main office to take cover, going over the protocol in his head; they'd practiced this many times. They also had the benefit of knowing the president's schedule, his staff's schedule, and the number of security personnel posted to each person and place within the White House.

The lieutenant was a young twenty-five-year-old, trained by the best of the U.S. military. When he found the president, he approached him from behind, just as he'd been taught to, then brought the man to attention, the gun pointed at the back of his head. He was still seated behind his desk, waiting for his security detail to come get him.

"Come with me, Mr. President." The young man's insides felt like they were turning to mush. He couldn't believe he was obtaining his target, the President of the United States, so easily. But his voice and stance were confident and demanding, as he'd been trained. There was no room for softness in this line of work.

The president stood up from his desk. His hands went up and he turned to stare at the lieutenant fearlessly.

"Do you know what you're doing, young man?" he asked gently. "Have you really thought about this, and the repercussions?"

The lieutenant's mouth firmed. "I'm just following orders, sir. Now come with me."

"Whose orders are you following, if I may ask?"

"You'll know soon enough, Mr. President."

Some of his other troop members met him outside the door, and the group moved to escort the president to the Oval Office. Smith looked around as they walked; the hall had been secured, and bodies lined the floor. They stepped quickly over the dead and rushed the president to the secured room. They had only five minutes to secure the White House, and needed to finish before any other military groups could be advised and react to their presence.

When they reached the room, they found that most of the White House staff was already there. Of course, World One had information on the meeting schedule, times, and attendees, and hadn't hesitated to use that information to gather the people they needed and kill the ones they didn't. Information like that was very helpful when you were trying to take over the White House.

Teams 2 and 3 were already securing their own targets at the Capitol.

***

Alfonso sipped his coffee and looked patiently out the window. He was calm and content, as his destiny was being played out all across America. For thirty minutes, he kept his phone off and listened only to the few couples around him. He wanted to be alone with his thoughts at this time, to gather himself for the shock of publicity that was to come.

The street outside was still. A few cabs sped by, but the lunch rush had just left, so Al was able to think in peace – at least for a while. He pulled out the small notepad he had stuffed in his breast pocket, slid his Montblanc out of the same pocket, and began to scratch down a few thoughts. This was going to be his moment, and he wanted to make sure that he remembered every damn word. He glanced at his watch. His men would be entering the White House now, and were probably passing all of the security gates without incident. Al and his team had spent years developing contacts and gathering intelligence on the White House, its security, and the staff schedules, to make sure that all ran according to plan.

His weapons had arrived earlier, and were now distributed all around America. He had ex-military men on his team, in charge of each local faction. They were responsible for all communication with their team and the "base" in Dallas. Gordo managed all aspects of these local teams, and Al trusted him implicitly; there would be nothing to worry about.

He had made sacrifices to get here, and had sacrificed others. He let his mind wander through the list of those who had lost their lives, and said a silent prayer for them. But he didn't dwell on that, as he had more important things to think about, like his mission. And he would accomplish it tonight.

Suddenly he sat up, pulling his thoughts from the past and thinking only about the future. "Fuck 'em," he mumbled under his breath. He straightened and worked to regain his original composure.

Glancing at his watch, he saw that it was time. He reached over and powered his phone back up, then motioned to the waitress with the international sign for the check. She reacted quickly, grabbing the check from her apron and rushing it over to him.

Good service, he thought to himself as he looked the waitress up and down. Her outfit fit her form tightly and he appreciated it openly, leaving all tact at the door. He shot her a sideways smile and threw the money on the table. When he looked up and stood from the table, his entourage had arrived outside the door. The limo stood open and ready to go. *Got to go in style*, he thought to himself.

Gordo was the first one to greet him. "Your chariot awaits, my friend." He shot Al a wide, toothy smile.

"Everything in place?" Al asked quietly.

"You bet your ass it's in place. Everyone's called in and they've secured their targets. You're up." Gordo bowed to him sarcastically and pointed toward the door of the limo.

In the distance, Al could hear sirens, but knew that it was too late.

Washington was his.

Chapter 33

"Jeff!" Lil was running toward him as soon as she hopped out of the cab. "Oh my God! Have you heard what's happening in Washington?" She was breathless when she reached him in the park.

Jeff could see two of the men from the cafe over Lil's shoulder, striding quickly toward them. Instead of answering, he grabbed her and started to run.

"What are you doing?" Lil screamed, struggling against him.

"We're being chased, Lil. No matter what, keep running. Those men back there were in the restaurant. They're the ones who tried to kill me."

"Oh my God." She looked over her shoulder and saw the two men in question. They were now wielding guns.

"Keep running!" Jeff shouted, pulling her back around. "Don't look back!"

Lil turned and began to sprint harder. "Run toward the police station. It's only two blocks from here." She could hear the men behind them. They were shouting, and gaining on the pair.

They paused when they came to a busy street and looked around; they had to cross if they were going to reach the police station, and didn't have time to wait for the signal to change. Jeff grabbed Lil's hand and charged out into traffic.

The cars whizzed by them, slamming on their breaks to avoid the pedestrians and laying on their horns. Jeff and Lil kept running toward the police station, the assassins close behind them.

"There it is." They ran full speed ahead for the station, hoping they would get there before the men behind them got across the street.

"Jeff, something's not right." Lil was the first one to see the front window. Two men were standing up front, with rifles pointed directly at the station officers. Two others were at the front door, apparently guarding against any other intruders.

Jeff slowed, putting a hand on Lil's arm, and the men at the door spotted them. They looked at the assassins crossing the street and gave them a sign, then looked back at Jeff and Lil.

"Shit," Jeff muttered. "We're trapped, and the cops aren't going to help us now."

Suddenly a voice shouted at them from a car in the back of the station. Chief Kouros was pulling around the building and heading straight for them. He screeched to a halt and threw open the passenger-side door. Jeff and Lil jumped into the car, and Kouros was speeding back through the parking lot and behind the buildings, into an alley, before Lil even got the door closed.

"Stay down," Kouros commanded as he sped through the alley.

"What's going on at the station?" Lil asked loudly, ducking down behind the seat.

"Hell if I know. But I intend to find out." Kouros spoke with determination and floored his Buick. "We're heading to my house, see if it's safe there," he muttered. "If it's not, I'm grabbing my wife and kids, and we're finding a place that is."

"How did you get out?" Jeff asked breathlessly. "Why didn't you bring anyone else with you?"

"I heard them coming, so I ran out the back. I could see the rifles from my office. My officers moved swiftly but they overtook our station. They've been trained, I'll tell you that much. These are no first-time offenders. And they'd scoped our office out before – they knew where the desks were, who was in charge, even where we kept the guns." He paused, thinking.

"I heard them talking before I ran out the back. You two are going to have to stay with me. They're looking for the two of you specifically, though I didn't hear why. And some of my officers are missing. I believe they're in on this. Whoever's behind this ... well, I'm sure we haven't seen the last of them." Kouros spoke quickly, his words rushed by the speed of the car. He ducked toward the steering wheel, urging the vehicle to greater speed, and came skidding out of the back alley onto the main highway.

Jeff and Lil breathed a sigh of relief as civilian cars surrounded them, and they sped toward safety.

***

When they pulled up to the house, Kouros jumped out to grab his wife and two young kids. "Wait in the car, I'll be right back. And stay down."

Jeff watched Kouros run up to the house. "What the hell is going on here?" he asked, turning to Lil. "They're taking over police stations?"

"Jeff, I've been trying to tell you. Whoever they are, they've moved into the White House as well. One reporter and a cameraman managed to escape as they moved through the building. I saw it on TV. They got off a brief message before their camera got confiscated. They showed some of them." Lil looked down as she tried to control her fear.

"Jeff, they have the president."

Jeff exhaled and closed his eyes, then heard Kouros yelling. Lil looked up.

"He's waving us in. Let's go."

Jeff and Lil jumped out of the car and ran into the house. Kouros and his family were huddled around the TV in their living room. Jeff and Lil could see the look of fear on their faces, and both looked toward the TV as well.

The image of a large, powerful man looked back at them. He seemed to be making some sort of speech to the cameras.

"My people, we have taken control of the White House. We have all local police stations secured as well. Do not fear." The broadcast was from the Oval Office.

Jeff's mouth dropped. "I can't believe this. That's Al Chord. He works here in Dallas. What the hell is going on?"

"If you wonder who I am and why I'm here, I'll tell you. Thirty years ago, I came to this country with a dream, a mission. My homeland has watched your government take advantage of you, and of countries less fortunate, for many years. And so we formed a plan, to take over and fix this problem. My father started this work, and I will continue it.

"I came here as Al Chord, but I stand before you as Alfonso de Cordova, son of Carlos de Cordova. It will do no good to try to resist. You have nowhere to turn. My organization is wide and deep, and I have your president and his cabinet here with me." The camera panned to the men seated on the couch. It zoomed in on the president, who sat tall and defiant.

The living room was silent at the Kouros house. The family looked at each other in denial, and Lil's eyes traveled to Jeff's.

"Right now there are no less than one hundred missiles pointed at your major cities," Al continued. "It could be your home. It could be your neighbor's home, or your daughter's. We are not playing games. Your United States has ceased to exist as you know it."

Kouros turned to Jeff. "We have to get out of here. I have some friends who have a collection of weapons. They're stored out by my cabin. We're going to need as much help as we can get."

"Let's go," Jeff muttered, moving toward the door.

Kouros grabbed his youngest daughter and ushered his son to the door. "Honey, grab what you need. We won't be back here for a while. We need to grab as many groceries as we can, too. Is the cabin stocked?"

"I stocked it last time we were up there – last month," his wife answered, nodding.

Within minutes, they were out of the house and rushing toward the car. They could hear sirens at the end of their street.

"Get in the car, now," Kouros yelled. "We can't be caught here!"

They all piled into the light blue Buick, along with some luggage and food. As soon as the last door was shut, Kouros floored the accelerator and squealed down the street. Just as they began to pull out of the driveway, a man stepped in front of the car and Kouros slammed on the brakes. Kouros pulled his gun from its holster and grasped it with both hands, pointing it through the windshield at the man in front of the car.

"Hands up!" he yelled. He dropped his right hand from the gun and threw the car into park, then reached over to open the door. His gun remained fixed on the man in front of them.

"Who are you?" he shouted, climbing out of the car.

The man calmly lifted his hands above his head. In his left hand was a manila envelope. He held it toward them, nodding toward the officer.

"What's in there?" Kouros snapped, his eyes still on the man's face.

"Help. I was sent by friends. Jeff should know."

Jeff thought back to his conversation with Stan and Victoria, and wondered how on earth the man had found him here. He jumped out of the car and ran over to the man to grab the envelope, then took several steps back to stand behind Kouros and his gun. Glaring at the man, he ripped the envelope open and pulled out the contents.

"Hey, ease up, I'm sent to help. Relax," the man muttered, watching Jeff.

"I don't trust anyone right now, got it?" Kouros barked at him. The sounds of sirens in the background grew louder, and Kouros and Jeff looked to their left to see police cars racing their way.

When they looked back, the mysterious man had ducked around the side of a building and vanished.

"Back in the car!" Kouros yelled. He took the car out of park and raced out of the neighborhood.

They passed three police cars with sirens blasting on their way out of the driveway. All three cars screeched to a halt as soon as they saw them pass by, then fell in behind them. Kouros skillfully led the chase out of his neighborhood. He knew the streets well, and took them on a ride through back streets and alleys. His driving skills outmatched those of the officers behind him, and he began to outrun the patrol cars.

As the other cars fell further and further behind, Kouros decided to head for the freeway. The roads were empty, with everyone glued to their television sets or battening down the hatches in their own homes. Kouros, though, looked in his rear view mirror, intent on defiance, and saw that the other officers were far behind them.

"One more turn through an alleyway, and it's onto the freeway," he muttered, slamming on the brakes again. He thrust his car into the next alley behind the houses, spotted an open garage, and backed his car into the open spot. Then he killed the motor and jumped out to close the door. The occupants of the car stilled, waiting for the sirens to pass by.

Jeff looked back down at the open envelope and pulled out its contents while they waited, bending close to see the papers in the dim lighting. The first thing he came to was a grainy black and white photo with a name written at the bottom: "Colonel Craig Cooper," he read out. "No phone number, no other information." He flipped through the package and came to another picture. Shocked, he saw that the picture had been taken when the subjects were deep in conversation; they hadn't known that they were being photographed. In the photo, Al Chord sat in a crowded restaurant, having a beer with none other than the Secretary of Defense.

Victoria and Stan were right. Al Chord's network reached a lot farther than anyone had realized. He held the photos out toward Lily, his mind reeling, and she glanced down. Her mouth fell open in shock, and her eyes widened.

Suddenly, a man threw open the door to the garage. "What the hell are you doing in my garage?" he shouted.

Everyone in the car jumped, afraid that they'd been caught. Jeff relaxed when he saw that the man had come from the house, not the street, and wore civilian clothing.

Kouros had come to the same conclusion, and approached the man. "I'm Chief Kouros, with the Dallas police department. The men you just saw on your television have also taken over the station. They're after us. I spotted the garage and—"

Before Kouros could finish, the man had grabbed them and was ushering all of them inside and up the stairs. "Then get in here. I'll throw a cover on your car. Stay quiet, and we'll make sure they don't find you. Damn foreigners. Think they can take over the whole damn country. This is the United States of America. They have no idea who they're dealing with..." The man continued to mumble as he closed the door behind them and left them in an upstairs bedroom. They could hear him making his way downstairs, and heard another door slam shut.

"Lil, Al must be behind Holly's disappearance," Jeff mumbled as his thoughts raced through the events of the day. "This was all about getting us out of the way, don't you see? He must have taken Holly to try to get to me. Bob was digging around in Al's business, and found out about the World One organization. That led to him discovering the list. That put all of our lives in jeopardy, as they probably didn't know who had the list. We're the loose ends. We've got to find her. And we can't let Al Chord get away with this. This photo is very telling. Al Chord is directly connected to the list that Bob found for World One. These organizations are directly linked. These photos show Al and the World One organization members together in a pretty chummy way. We've got a serious problem here. We've got to figure out what this lock box key is for and what this colonel's name has to do with anything. It's clear now that the Project Performance calls were just a ruse. This is not about Project Performance. Never was."

"World One is just a shell corporation to help Al run his dealings," she reflected. "Of course, it makes more sense. They weren't really concerned with Project Performance. That was merely to distract us from the real truth. That Al and Stan are connected and that this veiled membership list is the key to their plans."

She shook her head helplessly. "Jeff, what can we do? We're here, fugitives in our own town. And he's there, thousands of miles away, surrounded by his goons. You saw the list – it represented some of the most powerful men in America, and that list was long. Their influence has probably reached thousands of others. And now we know that this thing goes straight to the top." She gestured toward the pictures. "The Secretary of Defense, Jeff," she finished.

Jeff shook his head. "No one is invincible," he muttered. "You worked in DC for so long. You developed relationships with the president and some of his staff, right?" He looked at Lil and she nodded, her face unsure.

"Yes, but how does that help us? We have no idea who's on what side. The way they got into the White House, you know they have people on the inside – and probably more than just the Secretary of Defense. The point is, we don't know who all of the bad guys are. We know who's on the list, but there must be more than that, especially now that they have weapons pointing everywhere. No one can just waltz into the White House and take it over without a little help."

"Lil, the Secretary of Defense is really all you need," Jeff answered quietly.

Lil lowered her head, and he knew he had her. He also knew that he was right – the Secretary's name had been on the list of World One members, and now they had a photo of Al and the Secretary having lunch together. He had the clearance, and the access to vital defense information. He was the only link that Al had needed to get into the White House, find the people in power, and take them hostage.

"The president is a victim in this, so we can't count on him. But there are always back-up plans. There must be some sort of National Security team trained to deal with this type of disaster. Someone we can turn to."

This caught Kouros' attention. "Yeah, you're right – there's a special task force. I'm not sure what they're called, but they maintain their base outside of DC, just in case of this kind of security breach."

Jeff nodded, his hopes confirmed. "But how do we find them? And how do we get them to believe us? They don't know what we know about Al Chord, and that means that we have intelligence that could help them. But we need a way in; we definitely can't try to charge in there on our own."

Lil put her hand on Jeff's arm. "The president must know how to contact them. Maybe they've already been contacted, and they've set their counter attack plan in place. But they won't know who they're dealing with, and they don't know the number of spies out there. This list of members has law officials and DOD officials on it. For all we know, they have a spy in this security organization as well. They may be stopped before they can do anything."

Jeff shook his head as he listened to Lil. It was true, he knew. "How do we know who to trust?"

"Well, I'm sure we can trust the president. How can we get a message to him?" Lil asked quickly. "The president has a team on the ground there in the White House, ready for counter-measures in the event that someone tries to overtake the White House. I'm sure that they're underground, though, and not in the White House itself. They'll have to wait until they can get to him safely. In the meantime, we need to find out what we can do."

"You still have your cell?" Jeff asked quickly.

"Of course. It's our lifeline, remember?" she said somberly. The gravity of these words weighed on the group. Then she brightened. "Right! I have the president's phone number. He always carries it with him. And of course, he's got encryption – no eavesdroppers," she said.

Jeff nodded. He knew it was a long shot, but they had to try it. Al's people probably had the president's group surrounded, and it was unlikely that the president could answer a call, much less respond. But right now it seemed like their only option.

Suddenly Lil looked up with an idea. "We both have text messaging. If I send him a message, maybe he can read it discreetly. If he has it on silent, they'll never even know. It's worth a try, at least," she finished.

"I'll try anything at this point," Jeff stated, throwing his hands up in the air.

She pulled her phone from the backpack she had strapped to her back, paused for a moment, and then typed out a message. *Who can we contact for help? Lil*

The message was simple but clear. She looked up when she was done, exchanging glances with Jeff. Now they could only hope for the best.

Kouros watched them, then turned to his wife. "Turn on the TV!" he shouted. "Find out if they're still broadcasting. I'm sure the president is nearby – maybe we can see what happens." He pointed to a dusty TV located in the far corner of the musty bedroom, which appeared to have gone unused for years.

His wife flipped on the switch to find that Al was still speaking.

"My plan is simple," he was saying. "You stay where you are. Don't wander out. I am imposing a new law – a twenty-four-hour curfew. Do not try to break the law, as you will not live to tell about it. Members of my organization are everywhere, so there is nowhere to turn. Once all my men are in place, I will re-address the American public and give you an opportunity to go back to a new life. You'll like your new life. We'll put some order back into it. More security. I will do the thinking for you." The camera followed him as he stepped from behind the president's desk and walked over to the men seated on the famous Oval Office couches.

Seated closest to Al's new position was the president. He was still sitting tall and remaining calm, though his face wore a dangerous, dark glare.

"And if you value the life of your former president and his staff, you will do as I say. In twenty-four hours, I will address you again." He began mumbling something that sounded Spanish. Lil was a master at almost five languages, but she couldn't translate.

"What did he say?" Jeff looked to Lil.

"I'm not sure. Something about living together and dying together. He definitely doesn't speak a standard dialect. What's that supposed to mean?"

Jeff shrugged and turned back toward the TV. "Watch the president there, he flinched. Then he looked right into the camera." Jeff watched him intently. "Right there, wait, he's mouthing something into the camera. What is he saying? Aha, he's saying something about Baltimore. Baltimore Guard," Jeff blurted.

"The Baltimore Guard. Right, that's who we have to get to, then. But who at the Baltimore Guard can we trust? What if World One got to them?" Lil asked.

The camera panned away from the president now, and followed Al back to the desk. Apparently this distraction gave the president a chance to physically respond to Lil's text message.

The message was as simple as Lil's had been. "Baltimore Guard. Craig Cooper!" she shouted, looking at her phone. She looked up at the men around her. "The same name we received in the envelope! We've got to get to Baltimore. Who do we know that can fly us there? Al's team shut down the Dallas airport, but we've got to know *someone* with a private plane."

Just then the man who owned the house startled the group by opening the door to the bedroom.

"They're gone," he told them. "They drove right by my house. I think you lost them. But it won't be safe for long."

Jeff nodded. "Right. We need to get to Baltimore, sir. There's help there. We need a plane and a pilot."

The man didn't even miss a beat. "My brother's a pilot. He lives one block down. He's ex-military and I know he'd want to help."

"Let's go." This had become Jeff's mantra, and he needed one now; he was on automatic pilot. He had seen Victoria get hurt, maybe killed. He may have lost his best friend, Holly. And he wasn't about to watch his country be killed along with them.

Chapter 34

Stefano sat down on the bed and tore open a sleeve of crackers. He was working on his third sleeve, and getting pretty sick of waiting without any decent food. He didn't know how he got involved with this lunatic, but now there was no way out. There were members of the team everywhere, and Al had woven a wide and deep network of informants. He'd find him and have him killed in less than an hour if he ran.

So he waited. Not that things would go any better for him when Al got back. He was in trouble, make no mistake. He'd not only deviated from the plan, he was about to step outside of it entirely. He was surely dead either way.

The money was good, but he didn't know if it was really worth it, though now wasn't the time to develop a damn conscience. He finally ripped the crackers open, tearing the sleeve faster than he meant to, and sending half of them across the room.

He threw the rest of the crackers on the couch in frustration and stood up for the 100th time tonight to pace. Soon he would have worn a permanent path between the door and the couch, he thought. He'd been here for hours.

He stopped for a minute at that thought, and listened for any movement in the other room. It was deadly quiet. That worried him, badly. He was getting anxious and didn't want to have to deal with this anymore.

He opened the door and looked at her lying helplessly on the bed. Her hair was matted against her face, and her arms and legs were worn raw from struggling against the rope, but she was still beautiful. He stared at her, but she worked hard to avoid eye contact with him. She just stared out of the window. She hadn't made a noise since he'd brought her to the house.

"You are one pretty bitch." He walked to the bed and leaned toward her face.

She didn't blink, but stared past him out the window. She didn't acknowledge his words or his proximity.

"Don't ignore me, bitch." He backhanded her with one swift swing. She began to bleed from her mouth, where her teeth grazed her lip, and again where his ring caught her cheek just under her eye. The blood welled there, but she still didn't move.

"God damn it," Stefano screamed, walking to the bathroom to get a towel for her face. He threw it over her head, thinking that at least he wouldn't have to look at her now.

He stomped out of the room and slammed the door behind him. The force of the door slamming against its frame caused the windows to rattle unforgivingly, but he didn't care. If the mission was successful, there would be no reason to keep her alive, and he was ready to get rid of her. The whole mess was turning into a complete headache. He sat down on the couch by the phone, flipped on the TV, and settled in for the wait.

Chapter 35

The president still sat tall at the front of the room. He stood in at 6 foot 5 inches tall, and had a presence that filled any room, commanding respect with his size, stature and confidence. Even his voice, steady and strong, required others to listen. His courage was impressive in this catastrophic situation, and all of his staff looked at him with renewed respect and hope.

Over the last two years, the White House staff had been dragged through the media mud due to scandalous fingers pointing at their fearless leader. He had received scathing reviews from political wonks, predicting that his conservative stance would weaken his position on the economy. Taxes were high, the U.S. deficit continued to grow, and the president's voice had been noticeably quiet in a time of uncertainly. Markets don't like uncertainty or lack of leadership, and the media onslaught was on.

But now, in the face of such rancid evil, he stood tall and watched Al circling the room, looking at his group of hostages. For the first time in months, the White House staff believed that their leader had a plan, and that he was brave enough to follow through on it.

"It's a pity you're on the wrong side, people," Al said arrogantly. He walked around the couch and arrived directly in front of the president, giving him a sly, teasing smile.

"How mighty do you feel now, Mr. President?" he asked. "You have no more power, you have no more strength. You will wage no more wars against those countries less powerful than you. And the people around the world will see you for the weakling that you are. You are through."

Alfonso intended for his message to hit all of the people seated around the room, except of course for those who were on his side. And the man who had led them here. He hadn't been disappointed by this particular member of the White House staff's secret loyalty. The Secretary of Defense had come in handy on more than one occasion and had certainly showed his true colors in regard to his beliefs.

Now Alfonso shook his hand, grinning. "Mission accomplished. Now, if you will address your people, I have some other business to take care of."

As Alfonso stepped toward the door, though, a soft buzzing noise captured his attention and stopped him in his tracks. He glanced at Gordo, who shrugged his shoulders, and turned back around to face the hostages.

His eyes searched the former White House staff. They all stared back defiantly. Then he heard the noise again, and walked toward the group. It was coming from the president.

"Care to say something, Mr. President?" Al glared at the man, but received only silence. "Perhaps you didn't hear me." He walked toward the president and pulled him to his feet.

The phone fell to the floor with a thump.

"What the hell is this?" Al glared at his team and reached down quickly to pick up the phone. The text message was still in full display.

"Baltimore?" Al asked, half to himself and half to the president. "What the hell's in Baltimore?" He got no response from the president, and so turned to the Secretary of Defense. "Well?"

"There is a group of Plan B operatives there," the man responded. He glanced at the president. "The president has friends there, Al, and I imagine they are trying to regain control as we speak."

The president smiled, and Al swung around and glared at him.

"Don't fuck with me." Al shoved the president off his feet and onto the small couch, where the man landed with a heavy thump. His large frame shoved the couch backwards several inches, but his staff braced the couch, keeping it from yielding to their boss's large frame.

The president sat up and lifted his chin several inches. "This is the United States of America. Don't fuck with *us*." He stood defiantly, his large frame towered over Al's. Al, however, was enraged at his interference, and unmoved by his size. He lost it and swung hard, hitting the president squarely in the gut.

The other man collapsed with a gasp, falling to his knees.

"Gordo," Al demanded, quickly regaining his composure, "who do we have in Baltimore?"

Gordo was already on it, and had his phone out. "We have two teams of ten. And we can call in some of our other friends in World One." He had the phone in his left hand and the list of members in the other, and was quickly comparing information on the two.

"That's not enough," Al muttered, now pacing the floor. "These men will have been training for this type of situation, and they already know that we're coming. How soon will those missiles be ready? Have Sr. Gonzalez recalculate one target. Destination: Baltimore."

"Consider it done," Gordo replied. "It'll take twenty minutes to arm, maybe more to recalculate the coordinates, after they have their orders."

Al glared at Gordo.

"But I'll work to improve on that," Gordo replied obediently.

Suddenly another man ran into the room. It was the young team leader who had first retained the president. "Chief, a plane was detected leaving the Addison airport," he huffed breathlessly. He looked from his chief to Gordo and back, waiting for instruction.

"Shit, this is getting too sloppy," Al replied, tapping his head. "Well, shoot the mother fucker down."

"We put most of our team at DFW, sir," Gordo replied quickly, cringing at the news. This meant that they didn't have anyone to take care of a plane just out of Addison.

"We only had ground teams at Addison," the young officer agreed. "The plane is out of their range."

Al growled in frustration. "Well where are they headed?"

"We don't know, sir. They keep altering their course. We think they must know that we're tracking them, and be trying to avoid detection. But if I had to guess, sir..." The man paused and waited patiently.

"Well, guess," Al replied impatiently.

"I'd have to say the North East. I'm a pilot myself, and by the directly triangular path..."

Al didn't let him finish. "How many on board?"

"It's a small aircraft, sir, so it's hard to say. But there couldn't be more than eight passengers, with a pilot and a co-pilot."

"If it's small, it shouldn't take much to drop it out of the sky. Don't let that plane reach its destination," Al barked. He stormed out of the room.

***

Gordo had his contact at Edwards AFB on the phone within minutes, and two fighter pilots began fueling their planes in preparation for battle. Edwards had been one of the first targets of the World One takeover, and was now one of the most secure targets in the World One mission, thanks to some inside help. All the real fighter pilots were locked in one of the barracks, and replaced by World One employees. The organization would never have been able to buy all the real pilots off, and had chosen not to use them. These replacements were almost as skilled as the real thing, and had a far more secure base of loyalty.

It also helped that there was a missile capable of destroying 20 square miles aimed at the heart of their base. That fact had made the employees there slightly more ... flexible, Gordo thought, smiling to himself.

Beyond that, the base was surrounded by thousands of innocent people. The U.S. military would never sacrifice the lives of innocents in their own homeland, if they could help it. Al had known this and banked heavily on it. It had been a large part of the negotiations with the military men and women on base, and another part of their malleability.

Now Gordo meant to take full advantage of the tools and weapons at the base. Within a few minutes, his phone rang back. He listened intently, then rushed into the hall to catch up with Al.

"We've got two hot birds in the air," he told him quietly, looking down at his phone for confirmation.

Al nodded once in affirmation. "Good. I want zero communication while they're up there. Whoever's in Baltimore is probably listening, and may even be in contact with these people in the plane. I'm sure we have very little time." He turned and shoved his fist through a glass table in anger. The table held both vases and a crystal lamp, end everything fell to the floor with a crash.

"This is all going to hell," he muttered, his face dark and unhappy. People had become sloppy, allowing these kinds of mistakes.

Gordo put his hand on Al's arm. "Hey, we've got 'em, Al. And we've got control of all the major nerve centers in the country. This is what we've dreamed of."

Al shook his head, unsatisfied by Gordo's answer. "Track down whatever the hell's in Baltimore. In the meantime, I think it's time to make another address to people." He rubbed his hands together, as if he was preparing for a Thanksgiving feast. "And Gordo," he continued, "find out where the hell that truck is. We need to secure this place from top to bottom."

Gordo nodded and dialed his phone again. He looked out the window and saw a truck being hastily greeted by the lead team. "Good timing, guys," he said quietly. Perhaps the arrival of another team would calm his chief down.

***

It was now the security team's job to secure and maintain all points around the perimeter of the White House. Troops began to fall out like every other team deployment in a military situation. They swept confused tourists toward the West Wing of the building to secure the area. Heavily armed men swarmed onto the White House lawn, and few of them dragging missile launchers into the White House, heading for the roof.

When the truck was empty, the driver steered the vehicle around toward the guard gate, blocking off the main entrance. The truck then began to convert; bulletproof panels slid down over the tires, and another shield covered the windows of the cab. The driver jumped out and took a small remote from his pocket, punching the buttons on the remote to complete the transformation.

Gordo looked at his watch. The whole transformation had taken about three minutes. They had recruited the best the U.S. military had to offer, and it had been a relatively easy task. *It's a shame they pay their military so little,* he smirked to himself.

Chapter 36

Kouros huddled with his family, keeping still, trying to remain strong for them. Jeff and Lil sat in their chairs by the windows, watching for any movement on the street below. Jeff looked over at his partner and reached out to grab her hand.

"We'll be fine. Just watch." He tried to muster a smile but fell a little short. Surely they would make it out of this, he thought, but then he ran over the list of people against them. Very powerful people. And a country that hated them, it seemed. Did everything trace back to Al Chord and his home country, Cuba? Was there more awaiting them? What exactly were they up against? And were they the last hope?

His mind wandered involuntarily to Holly. His heart began to ache, and he squeezed Lil's hand. Holly was laying somewhere, alone and scared, without anyone to protect her. Was she hurt? Who had her? Was it the same man who had followed her and killed Jack? He thought of her smile, and for a minute he felt like he was back at the Brooklyn with her. Her face and her smile had lit up the room that night.

That thought brought Victoria rushing to his mind, and he felt a lump forming in his throat. The sight of her blood and her body slumped, motionless, was burned forever in his memory. Was she dead? Would he see either one of them ever again? Both women were in trouble, possibly hurt or dead, and he was unable to help either one.

"How much further?" he asked suddenly, trying to keep focused. It was important that he stay alert, he knew, and deal with what was currently going on, rather than what had happened.

"It'll be another two hours," the pilot replied. "I've been altering our route to keep them guessing as to where we'll land. I'll straighten our course just outside of Baltimore. That'll give them twenty minutes to get ready for us." The man paused. "It'll be the best chance we've got."

Jeff sat back in his seat and let those words echo in his mind. 'The best chance'... Well, at least it was something, he thought. He couldn't figure out how they'd gotten away so easily in the first place, and wondered if they were somehow being set up. They'd seen several troops blocking off the main entrances and buildings of the airport, but this man's hangar had been on a remote side of the airport. They had slipped in virtually unnoticed.

It had been fortuitous, but was also suspicious. Why had it been so easy? Where was the enemy? Were they being watched?

He was sure the men attacking the country were tracking them, and probably knew that they were in a plane. But what were they waiting for? He only hoped they made it safely to their destination. He knew that their best and maybe

239

only hope lie with some unknown entity in Baltimore. They were fugitives in their own country.

Kouros looked at Jeff, noting the desperate look on his face, and sought to draw him into conversation. "So, we know who began this. But how did he recruit so much support without being noticed? It must have taken him decades to recruit the people on that list. As long as we're sitting here with nothing to do, we may as well try to figure out how this happened."

"It's called World One, Kouros," Jeff answered quietly, thinking about the case Bob had been working on. It was all falling into place now. The man at the head of the textile company, his imports from Mexico, the Mexican accents during those prank calls all made it clear. "Al was behind World One, and World One hadn't wanted Project Performance to succeed. That had been their cover for attacking the law firm, which happened to be conducting their audience and handling Project Performance.

"And the U.S. anti-government sentiment has been on the rise both here and abroad. It was probably easier than we'd like to think to garner support for this kind of organization. Our firm had been tracking them for a while, for a number of different reasons, but we thought that they were a non-profit organization. They raised money for kids and fought for some specific political causes. That's why they showed up on our radar." He looked at Lil.

"Al's involvement in fighting against Project Performance seems to be a ruse. Bob's note to me indicates that he discovered Al was behind both organizations. If Project Performance had succeeded, it would have been costly for his company, because his hiring processes would have come under suspicion, but most importantly it was a distraction for our firm. And it was a convenient ruse to distract from his bigger plan. A bit of a poker strategy at hand. And the man just bluffed the country while he was taking the entire pot of money," Jeff finished.

Lil nodded and continued with what she knew. "We couldn't figure out why a non-profit charity group would be so close to the political system. Bob began to dig deeper into the organization. He had it figured out. It looks like it ended up costing him his life, but he sent me an email with everything he'd learned before he died. Stan Flemming was nothing more than a front man. I'm sure he made a mint keeping the press and organizations like ours off the larger organization's path. They talked about Project Performance, but never World One – likely to keep us all looking the other way instead of digging into their veiled membership."

"Sounds like Al Chord had something to do with Bob's death," Kouros concluded quietly.

"And probably Holly's abduction," Jeff added. He placed his head in his hands and rubbed his temples. He'd had a headache for what felt like the last week, and it was only getting worse.

Suddenly the pilot's voice broke into the conversation, capturing their attention. "Uh, guys? We've got company."

***

"Colonel, there are thousands of innocent people around here. Your family and my family live just a couple of miles away. You heard them; they've aimed their missile at Edwards, and that's only 15 miles away."

"This is what we've trained for, gentlemen. There is no room for interpretation of our procedures, and they are very clear. Collateral damage is something we've all been trained to expect."

"Yes sir." The young officer stood down and grabbed his cup of coffee. His hand was shaking uncontrollably, though, and he quickly set the cup back on the counter. He didn't want his boss to see that his nerves were shot. It was already a long day.

"We've got incoming," an officer yelled suddenly.

"Identify," the colonel yelled back.

"It appears to be a small aircraft, sir. A small passenger plane. Appears to be friendly, sir. It's private."

The colonel moved toward the radio and picked up the microphone. "Identify yourself. This is the United States Marine Base at Baltimore. I repeat, identify yourself. Over."

The radio crackled and came to life, with a Texan voice on the other end. "Yes, U.S. Marine Base, this is Ed Smiley. I'm carrying six passengers. We've been sent by the president to see you. Over."

"Sent by the president?" the officer repeated, looking sharply at the colonel. He turned around and focused on the radar screen.

"Sir," he called out, "there are two unidentified aircraft closing in on the smaller aircraft. It looks like they're under attack."

"Get two birds in the air, now!" the colonel responded.

"We've got two minutes, sir, what are our orders?" the officer asked, typing madly into the keyboard in front of him.

"Protect the plane they say was sent by the president. But get me the names of the people on that plane. I want to see who we're dealing with before we bring them in."

"Yes sir."

The colonel turned away from the radio officer and spoke to his lieutenant, going back to a conversation they'd been having before they were interrupted by threats and incoming aircraft.

"Get us back to this action, so that we know what's going on. Looks like this was an inside job, Lieutenant," he said. "There's no way you walk into the White House without having friends in high places. Find out who's on the take there, and fast."

He paused, thinking, then continued with further orders. "Tread lightly. We don't know who's on what side yet, and we don't want to be caught before we make a move."

The officer's eyes widened in response, and he pointed to a small TV on the desk. They'd placed the TV in the office when the ordeal began.

"We do now, sir." The colonel turned around and stood face to face with the image of the Secretary of Defense of the United States.

"My God," the colonel gasped. He regained his composure quickly and increased the volume.

The officers watched as Al Chord – Alfonso Del Cordova – walked back onto the screen. There were a number of cameras on the man, with what looked like the entire press corp in attendance.

The man took the podium, looked into the first camera, and began speaking. "Right now you are under twenty-four-hour curfew. Anyone found outside of their home until otherwise notified will be shot on sight. This is for your own protection. If you have any ideas of trying to reclaim the old government, and try to act on them, you will be killed. If you think about trying to defy us, we will find out, and you will be killed. We have no tolerance for retracing old history here. We are writing new history, where we will carry forward with the passion and conviction of a country fighting for renewed freedom. It is freedom from the capitalist pigs that have led this country astray and taken it into ruin. It will be great once again, if you stand with me.

"Your previous president will transition everything to me. He will then be exiled to an undisclosed location. Any attempts to help him or the previous government will lead to certain death," he Chord continued.

"We've got to get the president out of there, now," the colonel muttered. "I want our ground troops dropped off – by air – within twenty blocks of the White House. We have a deserted post at 20th and Commerce. That'll be our new command post." The colonel didn't hesitate. "I want the air unit to secure the area first. Clear the way for ground support."

He turned to another of the officers and barked out a new set of commands. "Get me a schematic of the White House. And get me the latest close aerial view of current activities out there. I want to see who and what we're dealing with, up close and personal."

The man in front of the radio screen turned in his chair, motioning to catch his commander's attention. "Sir, the migs aren't backing down on this passenger plane. They've locked onto the plane, and they're getting ready to deploy their missiles."

"Where are our planes?"

"Five seconds and counting."

"Fire at will."

"They're our own planes, sir."

The commander's mouth thinned. "Not anymore, officer. We don't know who's actually flying those planes, but I doubt that they're men loyal to this country. I repeat, fire at will."

"Yes sir." The officer repeated the orders to their fighter pilots, and watched the planes close in on the private plane and its followers. As the Baltimore planes drew closer, the man held his breath, his hand tightening on the controls. These were American pilots firing on American planes. It hadn't been done before, and it was certainly risky, regardless of the circumstances. Still, the migs were threatening a civilian plane, and that wasn't done either. When their own pilots were two seconds from their target, the migs pulled out.

The man breathed a sigh of relief, then frowned. "The migs pulled out, sir."

The colonel nodded once. He'd moved to stand behind the man, and had been watching the same screen. "Smart move. Have our guys escort our new friends in. Have them fully identify themselves. I want to see some proof that they're coming on the president's orders."

Within minutes, the officer handed the colonel a piece of paper. Scribbled on it were the names of all those on board the small plane.

"Well, I'll be damned," the colonel responded. "Jeff Michael Walker."

That name alone made the colonel trust the people on the plane. He had never met Jeff personally, but knew the name, and had read the files on Jeff's past. He knew that Jeff had worked with the NSA, among other agencies, until he left suddenly. When he lost his wife, he'd melted down, and the agency had asked him to take a break, with honors. The agency had continued to follow his path, and knew that he'd gone on to run a law firm in Dallas and live a somewhat quiet life. Given his past, though, the colonel wasn't a bit surprised to see him in the middle of this mess.

"Come on folks, let's go. Bring 'em in," he said to the officer at his side. "I know this name, and these people are going to be useful."

Chapter 37

Holly stared out the window. The pain in her leg and face was excruciating, but she refused to pass out. She wanted to stay fully awake around this guy, and she had other important things to think about.

She squinted to see through the slats of the blinds to the outside; where were they? She couldn't get up to see the outside world, but in her condition she couldn't have traveled far and lived. That must mean that they were still close to Dallas, maybe still in the city itself.

Her assailant had hauled her like a sack of potatoes, thrown over his shoulders, to a car parked in the alley behind her house. No one had been there to help her. The cops in the car at the front of the house wouldn't even have seen the kidnapping, since it happened inside the house and toward the back. He had taped her mouth shut and no matter how hard she'd tried, she could only muster a soft mumble. No screams to alert anyone.

She was beyond fear now, though. She was in survival mode, especially since it seemed that no one was coming to rescue her. It was all on her shoulders, then. She could see that it was bright outside, and strained to make out objects and signs. Based on the run-down wallpaper, bedding, and carpet, she thought that they were probably in a motel.

She didn't know what her attacker was doing, but she knew he wasn't happy. She could hear him on and off the phone in the other room, his voice shaking with agitation. Whatever was going on, it bothered him, and maybe that meant an advantage. She knew she didn't trust him, though, and that she needed to get away soon. If she stayed here, she didn't think she'd walk out of the hotel alive. She didn't know why he'd brought her here, but she didn't think it was for her health. That meant that she had to come up with a plan.

After nearly an hour of struggling against the ropes that bound her, she gave up, defeated. Her hands were bound behind her, and there was little she could do with them in that position. Her spirit continued to try to find hope, but with each passing moment, even she began to doubt that she'd ever see her family or friends again.

She closed her eyes and began to pray.

Then she had an idea. She opened her eyes and eyed the metal frame of the bed. It was just rough enough. Maybe. She sat up and slowly scooted to the end of the bed, where she lifted her arms behind her, with the frame of the bed at her back. She began rubbing the ropes across the rough metal surface, trying to fray the material that bound her.

Chapter 38

The president watched the man named Alfonso walk out of the room with his side kick. The man was a loose cannon, he thought, but he also believed that he could use that to his advantage. He certainly wasn't going to let this Alfonso get away with this ridiculous scheme.

He scanned the room to assess the situation; one of the Secret Service men was on the ground behind his desk, and there was another one down just outside the door. He could see the bottom of his shoe protruding from the hallway. The men and women seated next to him were putting on a brave face, but he detected small beads of sweat forming along their brows.

"People," he began to what remained of his cabinet. "It stops here."

The men and women around him nodded, happy to see their leader taking the initiative.

"Watch and listen. The United States of America is bigger than this house. It's bigger than us, and it's certainly bigger than this small office. Other generations must live on with the same freedoms we have enjoyed. We must stop at nothing to end this madness."

"But how..." replied his vice president.

"Watch and listen," the president replied. "If we remain cool and calm, we will have the advantage. These people are emotionally involved in their coup, and that means that at some point – in some way – they'll make a mistake. They care about this too much. If we stay calm, we'll see the mistake, and take advantage of it."

He stood up and started to walk toward the still-open door, finding one of Al's team standing just outside.

"Uh, sir, you can't do that," stammered the guard Al had left behind. "And don't get any funny ideas."

"I'm going to the jon, kid. You got a problem with that?" retorted the president.

"Well, uh, yes sir, I do. Al specifically told me to keep people from leaving the room, sir." The guard began to feel for his pistol.

"What, do we need a bathroom pass to go, for Christ's sake?" the president replied. "Or do you expect us to make a bathroom in this office?"

"Well, uh, just wait until Al comes back, sir," replied the guard. He grabbed his pistol and pointed it at the president.

The president moved to walk past the guard.

"Sir, uh, don't make me do this." The guard sounded more confident this time, and a little too ready to pull that trigger.

The president paused, holding his hands out in a calming motion. "Ok, kid, don't go crazy on us. I just need to take a leak. I'll wait." He turned around and assessed the room again. Only two guards, he thought to himself, and at least fifteen of his staff.

He looked at the news crew, thought for a moment, and then gave them the signal to start rolling the camera.

"Turn on the camera," the reporter mouthed in her cameraman's ear. "Something big is about to happen."

The president looked at the young woman standing beside the cameraman. He saw her whisper something to the man, and then saw the man bring his hand slowly up to turn on the camera. The president nodded at the woman. These were innocent people caught in the groundswell of drama, he thought. They weren't Al's people, and he might be able to use them.

While he had been walking toward the open door, he'd also noticed that the downed Secret Service man still had his weapon attached to his belt. Which meant that Al's men hadn't searched him. There would be another weapon hidden underneath his pant leg. *That's two weapons*, he thought, counting. If the other man still had his weapons, that was four.

The men and women of the cabinet, still seated on the couches around the office, watched their boss intently.

The president took his time returning to the couches himself. He stood for a moment, looking out the window at the world beyond the gate of the White House. It looked the same, and yet it was forever changed. The foundation of America's freedom, belief in capitalism, and belief in democracy were under attack. It was another fight for the right to be the United States of America. Left on this current path, the U.S. would fall at the hands of a dictator. He'd been in power for only a short time, but he was still a patriot. He wasn't going to allow the country to fall, and a plan was already forming in his mind.

The president was still standing when Al re-entered the room. The president heard him enter, but kept his back resolutely to the man and continued to look out the window.

Chapter 39

Their plane was met with a virtual army of military men, who whisked them away from the bird the moment it stopped at the end of the runway.

Kouros and his family were escorted to an SUV, while Jeff and Lil were shown into an unmarked military vehicle at the front of the line. They were driven to another building, where they found other people waiting for them.

The colonel greeted Jeff, Lil, and the group at the front door to the base. It looked more like a college campus than a high-security, last-front security base, but Jeff figured that was intentional, as a way to protect U.S. national interests.

The man in charge held his hand out in welcome. "Jeff Walker, I'm Colonel Craig Cooper. Welcome to our little military operation here in Baltimore."

Jeff nodded at the well-decorated colonel, then looked around and saw that they had entered a secret military world. All the buildings were unmarked and fairly unassuming. But it was clear that this was a very secure operation.

They were escorted immediately through the front office by heavily clad officers, and marched back into the base. Jeff was the first through the doors, and gasped at the blatant transition from neutral front-office greeting area to high-tech, hard-core military operation. There were few walls in the first expanse of building, making the outside of the complex deceiving. No one on the outside could see this airplane-hangar-sized unit, or imagine that it was here. Hundreds of military officers swarmed around bleeping, blinking screens and whirring computer terminals. As they walked further into the room, they saw that two screens covered the back wall from floor to ceiling. They were nearly two stories tall. One displayed a map of the U.S., while the other displayed a map of the world. In the center were various statistical data codes, along with a large, blinking red light. The LED display next to the light read: DEFCON 3.

When they were settled into the safety of the bunker, the colonel turned to Jeff.

"I know of your past endeavors, Jeff," he stated flatly. "You did some great work and we still train our new operatives with some of the plans you devised to retrieve intelligence. Good work."

Jeff nodded, pleased that his work was still being used, but didn't answer.

"Tell me," the colonel continued, "how the hell did you find yourself in the middle of this mess?"

Jeff looked up at the colonel, who stood a bit taller than him, and shook his head. "Well, Craig Cooper, I certainly know your name as well, and I'm happy to work with you. Hell of a mess we've got here. And how I got involved ... well, it's a long story, sir."

"Let's get to it, then. Follow me."

And the colonel led Jeff, Lil, Kouros, and his family deeper into the vault of the Baltimore operation.

***

Jeff took in his surroundings as they walked. He was re-entering a world that he had left long ago, and found it a bit unsettling. He was once again "backstage," in the guts of a military operation of the United States, back in the middle of the war zone ... this time standing between the United States and a man who had assembled an impressive array of power and money against them.

This particular base was an impressive display of technology prowess, dedication, and commitment. While Jeff was impressed with the fortress and the military team, he grew weary and impatient of the uncertainty. The reality of the situation was sinking in, and it was certainly amplified by the sight of the military presence before him. What had they gotten into? Considering the massive effort – over 6,500 people strong – Jeff knew that Al must have been planning this for years. He remembered the Al Chord he'd seen at charity banquets, interviews, business luncheons, and community events, wondering how the man had carried off.

He had always seemed harmless; egotistical perhaps, and a royal pain in the ass when it came to talking to him, but truly harmless. Jeff would have never guessed that behind that arrogant façade lay a man who was secretly planning to take over the country. He would never have thought that spoiled, haughty man capable of so much hard work.

He turned to the colonel, who had now joined them in a more private room. "What do you know about Al Chord?"

The colonel reached over to the desk next to him and picked up a folder. "Given your clearance, Jeff, I know you have the access for this file. This is what we know so far, about Chord and his operation. Let me know if anything there stands out, and whether you think we can act on it.

"The man appeared on our radar as far back as his college days at University of Miami. There were a couple of incidents there that caught our attention. First, he started an organization, made up of men only, that held meetings behind closed doors. According to some sources, their mission was to talk about Cuban government, and go through its values. Apparently these talks started to have a distinctly un-American flavor, and a couple of the members reported the group back to the administration. We got the call and began tracking his movements.

"There was never enough to tell us that he was anything more than a rebellious kid, though, so we put it to the side. Later in the file, you'll find that he started to move 'off the grid,' using cell phones less, communicating on the Internet less. There were fewer ways for us to track him, and we were forced to use visual tracking. This, of course, led to further suspicion – people don't go off the grid unless they mean to, and then they have a specific reason for doing so. A few years ago, when he purchased his own cellular network, we moved and sent in an operative."

"Operative?" Jeff asked.

"Yes, someone to watch the man and his operation. But this person's identity hasn't yet been revealed, and we must protect it. Especially now. That operative is our eyes and ears at this point."

Jeff continued listening as he began to read through the file. One thing was clear, he thought: Al had in fact been working for many decades to become untraceable. The colonel was right – there was only reason for that kind of move.

That brought them to today. According to the colonel, Mexico and Cuba had no less than one hundred missiles pointed at various strategic locations in the United States. One was, of course, the heart of Washington, DC. The others were the largest military bases across the country. For the moment, the United States was paralyzed by this threat, and the actions in DC. Even the president had been vulnerable to kidnapping. The troops in Baltimore had been untouched, due to a lack of World One information, and two hundred Baltimore troops were now in the midst of a brief about their planned counter attack in DC. The colonel's team knew of abandoned warehouses in the DC area, and thought that they would be adequately equipped for their needs.

Apparently, someone – at some point – had been paranoid enough to plan for this type of situation, and had made sure that DC would contain the weapons necessary to reclaim control of government. So there were plenty of resources in the city. The problem was getting to them undetected.

It was unclear how many enemy troops had infiltrated DC, but there appeared to be no less than one hundred people holed up in the White House. A few units had also been sent to other government buildings, like the Capitol. There were enough men wielding guns there that the senators and representatives were obeying their commands. Most areas had seen very little resistance to the invasion.

The Pentagon's capture struck Jeff with particular force. That was a very important – and secure – building, and should have had precautions in place against this sort of thing. Yet it was now under Al Chord's control. The magnitude of what that must have taken, and the possible results of such an invasion, reverberated throughout the halls of the military base. The fall of the Pentagon alone confirmed Chord's preparation. What else was he planning?

What was most interesting was that there had been distress calls from inside the government buildings. The Baltimore base had picked up a muffled cry for help, but the radio transmission had only lasted ten seconds before it was cut off. In the background were gunfire and then a loud explosion. With that, the line went dead. That meant that not everyone had given up. Someone there was trying to get out, and the hope was that this person had help. If they could find a way to work with people on the inside, it would make their job much easier.

Air units had been unsuccessful in their attempts to survey the damage so far. Two birds had flown close to the location of the Pentagon, but the perimeter was heavily armed with anti-aircraft missiles. The fly-by had been anticipated, and the return fire heavy; the survey had therefore been unsuccessful. Radar did detect some exterior damage to the northern-most wing of the crippled building, but they'd have to get closer to determine casualties and the extent of the damage.

The fact that Al and his team now knew of their existence in Baltimore would make the counter attack that much harder. Devising a plan to surprise Al and overtake his team would take the work of their best and brightest. Certainly achievable, but the odds were mounting against them. Their move was going to be complex, and required the element of surprise, along with a precision attack. The Baltimore team had its own elite force, which could be deployed as an advance troop anywhere around DC in minutes, if not seconds. They had choppers ready to go, and all of the teams were readied.

But the situation would get worse the longer they waited. Within the last hour, jamming signals had been coming from the White House to cripple all radar detection within a 500-mile radius. This limited the communication between bases, and forced Baltimore to send men out to retrieve information by hand and organize the counter attack with the military bases left. The colonel gave the order that the counter attack would take place at 2200 hours. He believed that attacking in the evening, rather than waiting for morning, would provide an element of surprise.

It also meant that it would be a very long day for the single set of troops in the White House. The Baltimore troops might find them fatigued, and getting sloppy. They were counting on the troops being weary and on the defensive. Plans were drawn up and the players put into motion.

Chapter 40

The president and his staff had been moved to a room in the interior of the White House, where there were no windows or doors to the outside world. The phones had been removed and the door was locked behind them. Outside the door, two heavily armed men stood guard in prison fashion. They wore the latest in underground military equipment and communication apparatus. They had also rigged the room with microphones so that they could listen to the men and women inside for pertinent information. They themselves remained silent, allowing no one to enter or leave the small room.

The rest of the building was a frenzy of activity. No less than twenty men had unloaded 1 ton of missile launchers, missiles, AK49s, and other weaponry in the White House, and now set about distributing the weapons to the men inside the building. Al planned to entrench his position and decreased the chances of a successful counter attack. These weapons would help steel their position.

He had anticipated some air presence from the intactive members of the military, though he didn't think that they would sacrifice the president, even if it meant saving the country. He loved their patriotism and loyalty, as misplaced as it may be. It served him well. He found that this patriotism often blinded them to the elements wanting to destroy them, as they believed that everyone loved the country as much as they did. There was no other explanation for how easily Al had been able to recruit and then overtake the government. Their sensitivity to political correctness, and protection of every group no matter their message or intent, ensured that Al himself had been protected, even as he sought to topple the government. While they may have kept an eye on *him*, they had turned a blind eye to his operations. Al knew he was good, but he also admired the U.S. military, and knew that they probably had a file on him big enough to fill the back of a semi-truck. Yet they had done nothing, for all these years.

And now it was too late.

In the West Wing of the White House, they were working around the clock to relay orders according to their plan and check in with their units across the country, making sure that each target was still secured. At this point, everything was in their power, but it was important to maintain that control; there had already been too many slips, and Gordo was going to ensure success.

Al Chord had assembled a well-oiled military machine, and he basked, only briefly, in the success so far. He had not, however, prepared for Baltimore, and that bothered him.

"I guess the U.S. had a card up their sleeve," he said to himself as he walked down the now-familiar hallway to the Oval Office. He was kicking himself; he should have planned for something like that, and the fact that he hadn't was a thorn in his side. Still, the show must go on; the cameras were waiting for him in the Oval Office.

In addition to the internal media for the White House, Al had invited outside media in DC and around the country to participate in this rather unusual press conference. He had extended these invitations to the press via his men and the armored cars he had acquired. Those cars had showed up at each media station in the area, along with regional branches for national media, to personally escort the reporters and their camera crews to the White House.

The press was always hungry for a story, he knew, and this would be the story of their lifetime. Every one of them was flattered to be invited to witness it, regardless of their loyalty to the country. Their passionate drive for the ultimate story overrode their wariness of walking into the unknown.

Halfway to the Oval Office, Al decided to move the press conference to the pressroom. It seemed fitting since this was, in reality, a press conference. He appreciated how the media was clamoring for the story. They were critical to his sharing his story with the country. The public and their media would learn to trust him as their new leader. And the world would watch as the mighty U.S. government tumbled. His people would rejoice and move freely in a country that had banned their commerce in the past. This would redefine the meaning of the land of opportunity. It was time for the U.S. population to know what was going to happen.

He stopped at the end of the hall to watch discreetly as troops escorted nearly one hundred press badge-adorned men and women into the press conference. They walked silently, obeying the guns being waved before them. Their faces displayed fear, anxiety, and excitement. This was history.

Just then, Gordo walked up behind him. "Everything's going according to plan, except for the little Baltimore thing. The troops around the perimeter are anticipating their ground attack. The vacant buildings within a 10-mile radius have been tapped. We will know their every move."

Al looked at Gordo and reflected on the plan. It was costly and hard had been work. This operation to take on the United States had cost him no less than $1 billion USD. Some of the money came from Al himself, some came from anti-government organizations, and some from Cuba, disguised in Mexican pesos crossing the border under the guise of the NAFTA agreement. The rest came from players hidden deep in the U.S. government itself. The conspiracy had gone to the very top. The very powerful Secretary of Defense had paved the way to the final destiny. They had given the vice president the promise of leading the country, but he'd kept his foot in both camps. In public, he professed loyalty to the president; in private he had cocktails with Al and his strategic team, and helped to orchestrate the single largest government take-over in the world's history. The president had, in the end, been surrounded by enemies. He – and the government of the USA

–never stood a chance.

Chapter 41

They walked purposefully toward the double doors, which were concealed from the main entrance to the pressroom. He could hear muffled chatter conveying an excited confusion from members of the press inside. As he neared the doors, he could also distinguish voices from the crowd.

"What do you think he's going to say?" a low male voice rumbled.

"I can't believe what's happening," an articulate female voice replied.

In response, several voices asked, almost in unison, "What exactly *is* happening?"

Al took this as his cue. With Gordo on his left and a young guard on his right, he thrust the doors open and entered the room dramatically. The members of the press hushed to silence.

He took long strides toward the podium, savoring the moment. He could feel one hundred pairs of eyes glued to his movement, and reveled in the glory. He'd been born to do this, he realized, and was absolutely going to fulfill that destiny.

One long last step landed him behind the podium, which was placed at center stage. He had asked that the U.S. flag be left behind the podium as a purely defiant and symbolic move, and grinned at the flag now. Then he turned to face his press.

"Welcome, ladies and gentlemen. I am Alfonso de Cordova and I am a Cuban-born American. I have been a member of your society for nearly twenty years. I have contributed to the wealth of this country with a successful business in Dallas, and have been your business partner, your neighbor, and your friend. I am not the enemy. Before you allow fear to enter your hearts, think long and hard about the state of your old government. Think about what your president, your House, and your Senate have done with the power that you had granted them. Scandal and misdeeds riddled the cabinet. I know you are tired and skeptical of this type of politics.

"Now we have entered a new era. You will go home and mark your calendars. This is the day that we changed history. Your government has ceased to exist as you know it." He looked to Gordo for confirmation that the cameras were rolling. Gordo beamed and gave him a big thumbs up, and pointed to one of the men filming the scene.

Al cleared his throat and continued. "And why? You must be asking yourselves why I would do this." He paused for effect, and became slightly emotional. "I will tell you why. With this change comes new hope for a global community. I have no interest in playing big brother to smaller and poorer countries. I have no interest in carrying the burden of those that cannot carry themselves. I am interested only in the well being of each nation on its own. We will celebrate our new life together. Cuba will reign and you will all see the glory of our country.

"What I will do is lead us into a new era. One where we will all prosper. One in which we will join with our other friends in the Americas, and will not be corrupted by the occupational nature of this former government. While it might seem now that we threaten your way of life, I'm here to help, and make sure that we all prosper. While I ask you for your support, I will tell you that it is not optional."

He scanned the room and looked intently at as many individual faces as he could. Some looked away, stunned by his probing looks. Others stared back defiantly. He could read people easily, and by simply scanning the room, he determined who would be the most dangerous individuals in this group.

"You have an opportunity to work with me to re-build this government," he told them quietly. "We will partner with other countries – countries your government has shunned in the past. The economic sanctions your government placed on my home country are despicable, and the only ones who have suffered are the innocent people of Cuba. No more." For one moment, his Cuban accent escaped him, and he paused to regain his English and his composure. "You are in no danger, as long as you listen and do as we say. If you do this, you will enjoy a new and very fruitful life.

"Opening trade with Cuba and strengthening trade all up and down the Americas will ensure a prosperous region. Your protectionism has hampered trade that would bring many billions of dollars of here to the United States." He smiled, knowing that this piece of information alone would get their attention. "I know that you are all very concerned about the national debt. You see it continue to rise and you worry about other countries owning a portion of your debt. You worry that some day that debt may become due. I am here to tell you that we plan to buy back that debt. We will not be owned by China or Japan or a group of wealthy families elsewhere. You will know who you answer to, and it will be me.

"You must know, however, that I have ensured your compliance. I am very serious about my convictions. Right now there are over one hundred missiles aimed at our top cities. If our new government seems in jeopardy at any time, the missiles will be launched; it's not important from where. I would recommend that you all remember this if you think about rebelling.

"Questions anyone?" He looked around the room and pointed to a man at the far right front row. "You."

"Guy Pierce, *Wall Street Journal*." The man stood, unwavering. He paused for a moment, then cleared his throat. "What are your plans? You think you have the team in place to run this country? Our military? Our congress? Are you thinking you're going to be the unelected president?" Guy clearly had more questions, but Al cut him off.

"Yes, Guy, I have read many of your articles about the scandalous behavior of your very dear president, who is now seated powerlessly just above your head. You have been very articulate on what is wrong with the government. Consider your position." Al looked around the room to make his point.

"Don't you believe that the country needs a new direction, a new goal? And besides, there is no looking back. Either you are with me or you will be held as a traitor against your new government. There will be no leniency. Justice will be swift."

He stared squarely into the camera to talk to the people of the United States once again. "I have men stationed throughout this country as well. If you think you will go unnoticed in your defiance, you are wrong. Let this be your one and only warning. If you join me, we will grow strong together. If you fight me, it will be your own death."

He looked around, having finished his planned speech. "Any other questions?"

Unexpectedly, from the middle of the room, came a soft but distinct voice. "I do have a question." A small woman worked her way up from the middle of the room, the people in front of her parting like the Red Sea. Al scanned the room and could see nothing but commotion from people moving to the side.

She finally emerged from the crowd, a petite, young, blonde woman. She was well tailored, from her pulled-back hair to her perfectly pressed suit. A hint of defiance and femininity was detailed in her slightly shortened skirt and the highlight of her brilliantly colored scarf.

"What exactly is on your agenda?" she asked, looking directly at him. "What will be the first change in your 'new' government?"

"*Our* government." Al looked down at this young woman and measured her, pausing dramatically. His organization was made up of men only. Women were weak, and he needed strength in his organization. In Cuba, women knew their place. He had tried to understand the role of women in America, but was still confused by their status.

He smiled condescendingly now, and waved her off. "Don't worry yourself over my agenda, young lady. I will ensure that I share the information I need to when you need to know it." He waved her back toward her seat, confident that he'd put her in her place.

She firmed her jaw, though, and continued. "You have not answered my question. Are you saying in no uncertain terms that you have no plan? I feel sure that with your apparent arrogance, you would revel in a question about yourself and your chance to display your superiority." She stood as tall as she could with her 5'2" frame and her voice remained soft, but her conviction was clear and rang loudly throughout the room.

Al smiled, and found himself immediately attracted to her. He noticed that her figure was visible in her yellow, form-fitting dress suit, and paused for a long moment, considering her. He anticipated that this silence would cause her discomfort, and force her to sit down. But after a minute she still stood, unwavering. He looked over to Gordo, and smiled again.

"Well, you will soon learn our plan. In due time, young lady, in due time. Now sit, before I introduce you to one of my staff." A man in a black leather jacket stepped from behind Al and flashed the rifle hanging off his left shoulder.

The young woman got the message and sniffed in dissatisfaction, but sat down nonetheless.

Chapter 42

When Holly awoke again, it was silent. After a few minutes, she started to piece together where she was and what had happened. She couldn't tell if she had been there for minutes or days, but she knew she had to do something. She had passed out praying for an answer to her escape. Now she listened closely to the next room, but heard nothing. She slowly raised her head to see out the slats of the blinds. Her eye caught a car door closing, and she heard the loud engine roar to life. She squinted closely to see that her assailant was outside, starting up his black Mustang.

She began to breathe more quickly as her heart raced, and the pieces of an escape plan started to come together in her mind. She watched him intently to be sure, but saw the Mustang spring to life and skid out to the small side road alongside her prison. That meant that she was alone, and it was time. She tried to sit up, but her head ached and it was hard to maintain focus. Swallowing heavily, she tried again, only to realize that her arms were now bound to the back of the bed frame.

Now she started to cry. Everything seemed hopeless, and she was tired of being by herself, hurt and confused. She struggled against the ropes until she could feel the burning in her arms. She paused, thinking of her friends and Jeff, then fought against the ropes with a renewed sense of energy, until she could feel them cutting into her arms. Finally – finally! – one of them began to loosen. She continued fighting until her right hand broke loose, blood streaming down her arm. She took a deep breath and brought it around in front of her, looking at the wound. Her vision began to blur, and she thought that she might lose consciousness again, but she turned her eyes back to the window and watched closely for her enemy.

With her right hand loose, she managed to sit up and spin around to release her left arm. Then she sat, motionless and heaving deep breaths as she tried to think of what to do next. She tried to stand, but pain shot through her right leg and she crumpled to the floor. She looked down to see that the bone in her shin was protruding sharply to the right; definitely broken, then. She took a deep breath and tried to think of a solution, then leaned up on one arm to drag herself across the floor, pulling herself slowly into the small living room.

She spotted her purse in the vinyl chair in the kitchen. With renewed hope, she pulled herself quickly toward the chair and grabbed her purse to see if her phone was still in there. If she could get her phone out and make a phone call...

Nothing. There was nothing in her purse. She looked around the room in disappointment, wondering where her attacker had put it. Had he brought it with them? Yes – she spotted the contents of her purse on the wood living room table in front of the TV. The TV was still on, with reporters talking frantically, but Holly didn't stop to listen. She reached the table and found her phone. Heaving, and dizzy from the pain, she transferred her weight onto the other arm and began to dial.

Chapter 43

Jeff and Kouros stayed in the briefing room while the officer's family and Lil were taken back into the cafeteria for some food and distraction. Jeff and Kouros were staring at the same screen, which showed a larger-than-life picture of Al Chord.

Jeff shook his head in disbelief. "Who does this guy think he is?"

"Hell if I know," Kouros answered. "More importantly, what is he really capable of doing? He sure seems to have a plan. I know the list you provided of the World One members was critical to helping the military here. One of the officers told me that they're in the midst of tracking down everyone on that list. At least that means we know who our enemies are now."

Two officers entered the room from behind them, and both Kouros and Jeff jumped at the sound of the slamming door. They spun around to see the two officers, heavily decorated, entering the room. A third and much smaller man opened the door behind them and stepped in as well.

"Gentlemen, I would like to introduce you to Colonel Ryder and General Biding," said the smaller, younger man, who appeared to be in army fatigues.

"Gentlemen," said the general. He reached out a large, weathered hand to shake Jeff and Kouros' hands.

"Quite a mess," Kouros finally said, at a loss for words.

"Yes, sir," said the general. "What can you tell us about all this?" He looked from Jeff to Kouros, then took a seat with the colonel. The smaller man continued to stand behind them, watching the conversation closely.

Jeff began, glad to be of some service to the men saving the day. "Several months ago, my business partners and I started getting very close to an organization called World One," he said. "World One appeared to be a non-profit organization supporting youth programs, but straying more and more into the political fray in equal rights issues. This caught our attention. My partner Bob started to uncover some inconsistencies..."

"What kind of inconsistencies?" the general asked.

"Stan Fleming was all over the papers, a real front man. He talked a good game and looked the part, but he sure didn't seem to run very deep. The more we dug into his background, the more we realized that we couldn't determine how he even got into such a prominent role. Records on him were difficult to find, and there were so many dead ends. We found the university he'd supposedly gone to, but when we called the university they couldn't find any records on him. Things like that."

He leaned back in his chair and ran his hands through his hair, realizing that he hadn't had a hair cut in over a month. He was used to having it cut close over the ears, a little longer

278

in the front ... now it was over his ears. *Just another sign of how much things have changed*, he thought ruefully.

"As Bob started talking to more contacts, I guess word got back to people who didn't like us asking questions. Bob began getting threats. He was getting too close to the truth of the membership and the mission of World One."

"We know about your partner, Bob, and we're very sorry," the general said quietly. The smaller man handed both the colonel and general folders, which they opened.

Jeff could see over the top of the folders that they were looking at a picture of Bob Wright. His throat tightened and he took a deep breath, trying to remain calm and rational. Now wasn't the time to get emotional.

"So where does Al Chord come in? When were you introduced to him?" the general asked both Jeff and Kouros.

Jeff turned to Kouros, then back to the general. "Well, after talking to Kouros here, I recalled representing Chord in a trade dispute. There was nothing particularly stand-out about the case, but then we found out that Bob had new information, and had actually tried a case against Chord's company. He was uncovering some activity that may have been unfair trade practices. He had asked for an audit of that company. We knew that Chord wasn't happy about it, and that he was hiding something. That's about the time the shit started to hit the fan."

He paused, gazing at Kouros. "We're still trying to wrap our minds around it, to be honest. I knew Chord socially; we were in a little of the press together, and back then he seemed to be just another shrewd businessman. But with the information Bob uncovered, and then the threats, and Bob's death..."

"Well, this certainly didn't happen overnight, and it seems pretty well orchestrated," the colonel noted. "You two are damned lucky to be sitting here right now, and we're damned lucky that this Chord fellow isn't powerful enough to reach us here, yet." He looked at the general with a frown, and a thought seemed to pass between the two men.

"What do we do now?" Jeff asked.

"Share everything you know about Chord and the rest of his team with Mike here," the general said, pointing to the smaller man at the back of the room. "We'll be back in touch." With that, the general and colonel stood and were gone.

Jeff looked down at the floor below his feet, wondering what they would do next, then jumped. The phone in his pocket was ringing.

Chapter 44

Stefano had gone for a long drive to try to clear his head. His prisoner was still sacked out in the other room, safely tied up. With that broken leg, she didn't have a chance of going anywhere.

He'd been watching the news when he saw Al on TV. It had been quite a shock, and he still couldn't believe what he'd seen. He had leaned closer to the TV, staring at his boss, and had finally decided that he had to get out and think. He'd had no idea that this was part of the plan, and wasn't too pleased about it. Yeah, he had his issues with the U.S., but it was the best place on earth to live. His family had opportunities here that they never would have had at home, and they'd become Americans. They loved this country. Now he felt a pang of regret, thinking of how his mother had warned him about getting involved with the wrong crowd. She'd certainly been right, and he should have listened to her.

This had thrown new light onto his mission, and the things he'd been doing over the past couple of days. He hadn't been happy with the assignments, and he'd already been questioning his commitment. Now he wondered if he wanted to hold the woman in the other room hostage for someone he knew to be doing something so stupid.

When he looked up, he realized that he was on the outskirts of Dallas. He must have been driving for over an hour, lost in thought. Now he snapped to and realized that he'd better get back to the motel. And he had a plan; Al was going to have his ass, no matter what happened. The incident at the diner had put him at odds with the chief, so there wasn't a chance in hell that he was getting out alive. As far as he could see, though, that meant that there wasn't much downside to going against the boss. And now that he'd seen Al on TV, and knew what he had been planning to do, he couldn't see another way out.

He turned the car around in the middle of the road, coming close to hitting some of the oncoming cars, and gripped the wheel tightly. *I can't let this happen*, he thought. He stomped on the gas and steered back toward the motel and the girl.

"Dead if I do and dead if I don't, most likely," he said to himself, going through all the possible repercussions of his new plan. At least it gave him a shot at a quick getaway, and the girl a shot at being saved.

Chapter 45

The president looked down; his mind was already racing to his next move. He took a deep breath and a couple of steps forward. He could hear footsteps coming down the hallway, and feel the nervous energy from his cabinet, which stood just behind him. He recalled his military training and knew that it would kick in when it needed to; that was more dependable than his brain, right now. With that last thought, he closed his eyes and focused. When he opened his eyes again, he could see Al's team of thugs coming into the room toward him.

As they reached out to grab him, he jabbed his right hand, fingers extended, into the eyes of the man in front. His left arm immediately swung around, boxing his opponent on the right temple and knocking him off his feet, his hands thrust to his injured eyes. The president whirled around to the man on his right and kicked his shin sharply enough to make the man crumple. As the man leaned down to reach for his leg, the president grabbed the gun out of his right hand, and stepped back, gun pointed at the three men.

"Down on the floor, now!" he barked.

The three men grunted and gasped in confusion. The one man left standing dropped to the floor without hesitation.

As the president breathed out in relief, the young leader of the group stepped into the room. He looked down at the men in front of him, then back up at the president, who instinctively shot in his direction. The man, eyes wide open, darted to the left to hide behind the door, where he shouted for backup.

That meant that they didn't have much time.

He turned to the men and women of his cabinet, handing the gun over to his Secretary of Energy.

"Keep an eye on them," he muttered.

He leaned down and stripped the men of their weapons, then stood up and distributed the guns to his own staffers. He sneered and barked at the Secretary of Defense, who was now tied up and leaning on the wall in a corner at the back of the room.

"Fine mess you created here, Stan! What the hell were you thinking?"

He walked slowly to the corner, where the secretary was sitting, reached his hand back, and hit him in the jaw with the butt of the gun. The secretary grunted in pain.

"That's for the country," the president exclaimed. He punched him on the left cheek with his other hand. "And that one's for me."

Then he stood and walked away from the bleeding man, his eyes roving over his cabinet members. "People, you know the plan. Cover me."

"Sir, let me," the Chief of Staff interjected. He had a gun from a downed man and pointed it toward the doorway, stepping quickly into the open space. With one last step he swung through the doorway and to the left, pointing the gun in the direction of the young opposition lead. He pulled the trigger, and a shot rang out. The sound of the young man's body hitting the ground echoed through the hallway, and the other cabinet members breathed out in relief.

"Four down," the president mumbled, moving toward the doorway.

They could hear footsteps coming toward the open door from the hallway, and the Chief of Staff swung around to face the new intruders. He got off four more shots, each reaching their targets, before a bullet found him. It ripped through his right arm, and the force of the hit swung his body around and back into the room. The gun flew out of his hand, sliding across the floor to the back of the room. Another one of the cabinet members ran to the gun, while someone else ran to the Chief of Staff, grabbing him around the torso and spinning him around to drag him back into the room behind the couch. He laid him on the floor and stood up with his own gun, then spotted the president – precariously close to the open door – and ran in front of him.

The two men paused when they realized that the shots outside the room had stopped. The hallway was quiet. Too quiet. They both kneeled quickly, training their guns on the open door. The men behind them, and the lone woman, took their places behind the president and his partner, ready for the attack. No one dared breathe.

Chapter 46

Holly took a deep breath and placed the phone back in her purse. She looked around the room; it was a pale green, with dust lining the lampshades and windowsills. Perhaps it had once been a vibrant green, she thought, but the dust had covered and muted its original color. That didn't help her figure out where she was, though, and she moved on.

She was sitting on the floor, but could feel the pain throbbing through her left leg. She wouldn't be able to walk on it, she knew, and if there were stairs they would prove difficult. Beyond that, she didn't know where she would go once she got out. She certainly couldn't walk anywhere, and she didn't have a car to drive. Jeff had told her not to call the police because they couldn't be trusted, but what did that leave? He hadn't been able to give her any usable information, or suggest anything solid. She took a deep breath, fighting off the feeling of helplessness.

Just then she heard a car door slam from outside the motel room door. She gasped and cradled her purse to her chest as she dragged herself back toward the room where she had been held prisoner. Maybe she could get back in there and hold him off for a while. Maybe Jeff would send someone to help her. She was halfway across the floor when she heard the motel room door swing open, crashing loudly against the wall.

"What the hell?" she heard the man say, in what sounded more like amazement then anger. "Where on earth do you think you're going?" he asked quizzically.

Holly finally stopped and began to sob, overcome with fear and exhaustion, and the defeat of being caught. Again. She crumpled into the floor and let the tears come. She'd been awake for nearly twenty-four hours straight, holding her breath in fear the entire time. She'd been attacked, injured, and kidnapped, and had spent the last several hours in severe pain. She was now completely exhausted. She could feel the hope leaving her body, and she was tired of staying brave.

To her surprise, the man reached down and carefully lifted her into his arms. He carried her over to the couch, and set her down gently. She stared at him in confusion.

"Yeah, I know," he said, walking back to the kitchen in the tiny motel room. He grabbed a glass, filled it with water, and walked back to hand it to her. She reached out for the glass but held it without an attempt to drink.

"Drink it, go on," the man insisted.

She closed her eyes and lifted the glass to her lips. She could feel the dried blood on the corner of her lip, and sipped the water slowly. When she was done, she smoothed the water over her dry lips. She instantly felt the cool liquid energizing her body.

"Now, what am I going to do with you?" the man asked, sitting down in the chair opposite her. He just stared at her for a second, then shook his head.

"Do you know what this fucker is trying to do?" he asked suddenly. "He's trying to take over Washington, DC, the fucking loon." He reached both hands up to rub his eyes. "They never told me that," he added, sighing.

He sat there for a long time in silence, and Holly looked at him, trying to understand what was going on. He still had his hands over his eyes when she said, "Please just let me go."

He looked at her with wild eyes, then shook his head and placed his hands over his face again.

"You need to go," he finally agreed. "I don't know how you're going to walk on that leg, though." He thought about this for a minute. "Can you drive?" he finally asked.

"Yes, yes, I can drive."

"Sudden fucking conscience," he gasped. "Guy who hired me is a fucking nut case. He's in Washington, DC now, got the damn president held hostage in our own White House. Fuck 'em, I don't play like that. This is a good fucking country. And I'm not going to do his dirty work for him if he's that kind of guy."

Holly glanced to the TV, where the man was pointing. There she could see a man standing in the pressroom where the president and his press secretary normally stood, speaking.

"Shit," she managed to say.

"Nut case," Stefano said again.

Chapter 47

Jeff hung up the phone and felt his heart hammering away in his chest. How on earth was he going to get to Holly, and make sure that she was safe? They had been able to track her cell phone signal to within 100 feet of a small industrial park area on the south side of Dallas.

He rushed through the complex to find Lil as soon as he got off the phone.

"Lil, Holly called, she's ok. She needs our help. Who can we trust in Dallas?" he muttered.

"Why don't we call Jane?" she mused. "She's probably still there, and she knows Holly."

Jeff thought about this; he didn't like pulling his secretary into the middle of it, but he also didn't see another choice. She was probably still in town, and how much worse could it get for anyone? There was a nut job in DC trying to threaten the United States. This called for everyone to step up.

"Ok, get her on the phone, and we'll talk her though this. Doesn't she have that bouncer boyfriend, what was his name..." He thought for a minute. "She could bring him with her."

"And bring firepower..." Lil added.

She dialed Jane's number on her cell phone and brought it up to her ear. "Jane, hi, yes I know ... It's terrible ... Yes, yes,

I did see it on TV, let's talk about that later. Right now we really need your help."

Jeff watched as Lil relayed to her where Holly was and how to get there. She was to go to a safe house just outside of the DFW airport, close to Carswell Air Force Base. The base had been closed in 1994, but remained a reserve base, and still had military personnel. They were hoping that it was a small enough target for Chord to have forgotten about. The colonel said he knew some folks he'd joined with down there, and that they would keep an eye on Jane and Holly.

"Bring muscle with you, Jane," Lil cautioned. "These guys are dangerous, and I'm so sorry to ask you to do this." She listened as Jane replayed what she was asked to do. "We have no other choice," Lil added.

Just as Lil was starting to hang up the phone, two junior officers rushed in and ordered her and Jeff to leave with them. They left no room for discussion, so Jeff and Lil grabbed their things and walked after the men, confused.

"We have incoming," one reported as they marched Lil and Jeff down another hallway, behind the big screens and whirring computers. They stopped at a door, swiped a card, and leaned forward for a retina scans. When they were finished, the back wall opened to reveal another set of hallways. They took Lil and Jeff down the left hallway, lit dimly by side emergency lights.

Soon the joined Chief Kouros and his family in a side room with the colonel and his team, while the rest of the officers and staff were taken to a room in the back.

The colonel turned to Jeff. "It appears enemy craft are headed our way and hot; they got off a few rounds before our team got out there. Our birds are in the air and will get 'em, hang tight."

"Please remain calm," the officers told the people in the room. There was a small refrigerator, a TV showing re-run movies, and a couple of board games scattered on the old wooden table. Jeff and Lil exhaled at the same time, each coming to the conclusion that they were going to be here for a while.

Before the officers spun around to leave the room, Jeff jumped up, remembering Holly. "Excuse me, but what about my friend?" he asked. He told the colonel about his conversation with Holly. The colonel immediately got the trace on the phone call and sent a team out to secure the target.

"Sit tight, Jeff, we'll get on it," the colonel reported, then left the room.

Before Jeff could follow him, a junior officer turned. "The colonel asked that you stay with us until the air has cleared, sir."

The room fell silent when the door shut, and the only sound was that of the locks securing the door behind them.

"Sir, we know where she is," the junior officer continued. "The safe house is ready for her, and if your friends follow your instructions, they should be safe. We're keeping an eye on them," she said flatly.

Jeff walked back to where Lil was sitting. He felt relieved knowing that they knew were Holly was and that Jane was on her way to help, and that soon they would be safely at the base together.

"Hold on, Holly."

Chapter 48

Holly took another sip of the water her captor had given her and glanced at him over her cup. He was still mulling over what to do, she thought. He pointed to the TV, and her eyes shifted back to the images on the screen. She looked at Al Chord again, but couldn't believe that he and his thugs had been able to break into the White House. How in the world had they gotten past all that security?

"Lunatic," the man said finally, after a long silence. "And for me to say that is really saying somethin'."

She shifted her attention back to the man. "How'd you get into this?" she asked.

"Forget about me. You have enough to worry about," he said distantly. "As for your question, though, all I can say is that it's a living."

"Some living," she responded, looking at him and his dingy shirt, unshaven face, and worn-out tennis shoes. Then she looked around the motel room that had been her prison for the last twenty hours or so.

"Shut the fuck up," the man retorted. "Shut up, before I change my mind." He ran his fingers through his hair, then rubbed his unshaven face. "You got friends or somethin'?" he asked.

"Yeah, you killed one of them, you fucking asshole." She felt her face redden as the images of her friend Jack came rushing back to her in a wave of anger and sadness.

"Yeah, well, you could be next. I'm not your friend." He looked down at the ground and shook his head. "Listen, you're going to need some help getting out of here. You might be able to drive, but you ain't got a car. Do you have friends?" he repeated.

"Yeah, I got friends," she said blankly, still grimacing from the pain from her leg.

"Well, you oughtta give 'em a call," Stefano said. He grabbed her phone off the coffee table near her purse and threw it to her.

Then he stood up and grabbed his jacket from the back of the couch. "Good luck." And with that he was gone.

***

Holly looked down at her phone and began to dial, looking around the room and out the open door to make sure she was really alone. She listened to the phone ringing, and on the fourth ring, sighed in relief.

"Jeff..."

Chapter 49

The president and his cabinet remained still, pointing their guns toward the open doorway. Still, silence reigned in the hallway. The president could feel his heart pounding, and he focused on remaining calm. *Focus on the enemy,* he told himself. *Anticipate when he's going to show up.* He listened closely and looked into the hallway for shadows or reflections in the window in the hall. Nothing.

Apparently the enemy had fallen back to regroup. That made him smile; they obviously considered him armed. And dangerous.

"Cover the door," he whispered to the men closest to him. He slowly stood up and surveyed the room. There were several doors leading from this room; the president had spent a lot of time here, and he knew them well. None of those doors led to the outside world, though, and each might have a guard behind it. What had once felt like an open and welcoming room had suddenly become his prison. He surveyed the doors to the East Room, the two hallways, and the Blue Room, trying to think, then walked slowly around the room, testing each door. Only one was unlocked – the one that opened to the hall leading to the Blue Room.

He walked to the back of the room and stood to the right of the door to the East Room. He knew that if he could get through that door and out toward the East Gate, he may be able to find the long-unused and thus little-known underground tunnel to the left of the entrance. The tunnel had been built in 1948 when, under the guise of reconstructing failing structures, Harry S. Truman oversaw the rebuilding of the exterior frame from wood to steel structures. At the same time, the underground tunnels were dug and expanded for times of emergency. They were much the same today, though they were used only rarely.

They would need to create a distraction, he realized. He looked around the room and then down at the fallen enemy, who was lying beside the open door. They had stripped him of his weapons, but he wondered if the man's body held anything else of value. A hand grenade perhaps, or something else. He walked over to the body, his gun still pointed toward the open door, and leaned down to check the man's arms, waist, and legs. When he came to the man's right calf, his search paid off. The president held his breath in excitement until he saw that it was nothing more than a pack of smokes and a lighter.

The president sniffed and laughed to himself. He'd quit the stuff years ago. This was no help

He pulled the pack from the man's sock, though, and stood, his thumb flipping open the lighter and clicking the switch. A bright flame jumped up from the tube. It worked, then. That would need to do.

"Men, we're going to have to create a distraction," he muttered. The men around him nodded in response. They still

298

held their guns trained on the door, but watched him out of the corners of their eyes.

"Bob, with me," the president barked quickly, taking on his military persona. "The rest of you, continue to cover that door." He looked around the room again as he spoke, then grabbed a chair and pulled it toward the door, grunting to himself. The men straightened as he neared, focusing their attention on any sound in the hall. There was nothing but silence outside of the door, though, and they looked back to their leader.

The president put the chair in place, tore some material off the bottom, and pealed it back to pull out some of the stuffing.

"Men, on my mark, cover this door, and when I get out the back door, follow me." He looked up, waiting for the men in front of him to nod their understanding. "We need to get word to Maryland. They'll send some boys to help."

He leaned down again and flicked the lighter a few times, encouraging it to burst into a tiny flame. Once it did, he lifted the flame to the stuffing from the chair cushion, and jumped back as the stuffing caught. A column of black smoke rose from the material, hitting the ceiling and spreading quickly. He covered his mouth, coughing from the smell, and ran with Bob to the back of the room.

It was quick work to shoot the door lock, and a moment later he was flinging the door open to find an unsuspecting guard standing on the other side. The president pointed the gun at the man, who held up his hands.

"Wait, sir, it's Chester. I've worked here for thirty-five years, sir," the man pleaded.

The president took a deep breath, realizing that this man was not the enemy, and pointed the guard back into the room with the rest of the cabinet. "Get in there and help them get out," he snapped.

"Thank God, sir, nice to have you back," the guard responded, grinning.

The president nodded, but moved quickly on to the reason for his appearance. "Help us–"

Before he could finish his sentence, Chester had pulled his gun and was pointing it toward the outside door of the East Room.

"Run," he yelled, just as Al's goons burst through the door.

The president and Bob sprinted for the back of the East Room, finding the door that faced the East Gate. They slowed down just long enough for the president to lift his gun and shoot out the lock on the door, then rushed through the door as it swung open.

From behind them, he could hear shots ring out and cries from downed men. He and his partner didn't pause for the wounded, but ran as quickly as they could to the side of the building, just beyond the second hedge. There they found a door to what appeared to be a basement. The president shot this lock out as well, along with the chain that held the two angled doors together. He reached for the right door and thrust it open, then stumbled down the stairs to the tunnel below.

The Secret Service had trained all of the cabinet on what to do in such extreme circumstance, but they never really thought they'd use it. Now the president shouted his instructions to Bob, hoping that the man remembered his training.

He heard steps behind them and hoped it was his other cabinet members, rather than members of Al's security force. The door slammed behind them and he increased his pace, Bob on his heels. Together, they raced down the cold, dimly lit tunnel toward freedom.

As they neared the door at the end, the president reached into his pocket and pulled out his ID card. He held it before his face, praying that the reader on the door would recognize the barcode on the card. He heard the click and rushed through the door, surprised to find that the reader still worked. To his greater surprise, he crossed through the door to be greeted by two armed men. They appeared to be military men, and immediately stopped to salute him. Another pair of men joined the first from the other side of the tunnel. The door closed behind them.

"This way, sir," one of the men muttered, leading them further into the tunnel.

"Who are you guys?" the president yelled, realizing abruptly that he may have found his way back into the enemy's hands.

"Sir, Code 22, sir," the man answered, grinning.

The president grinned back, relieved. That was the code name of their escape plan, which meant that these men were friends. They had trained for Code 22 for weeks, and had just executed it perfectly. "I'll be damned," he said. Then he thought of his cabinet, still racing toward safety. "The rest of the team is behind us," he yelled.

"We got it sir, but right now we need to get you out of here. Faster sir," the man yelled.

The president had begun to feel his fifty-eight years and was slowing, taking deep breaths to keep up with the twenty-something military men. He looked up at the end of the tunnel, saw a football field-sized hangar, and gasped in shock; he had been in the White House for over two years, and had no idea what lay underground in the back yard.

Sitting in the middle of the opening was a big, orange circle. Sitting in the center of that was a vehicle that looked half jet and half helicopter. *Definitely military*, the president thought. He wondered how many billion-dollar military crafts had been purchased, and whether he'd signed off on this one without even realizing it.

"We couldn't tell you about it, sir," the man finally said on his right. He'd read the president's surprise, and guessed the reason. "For your own protection, sir. Come this way please." He directed the president out to the waiting craft and escorted him into the plane. "Hold on, sir, it's going to be a helluva ride." The man stepped away as the president stepped into the open door of the craft.

Another man already onboard handed him a helmet with a microphone on it. The pilot looked back, waiting for the thumbs up.

"Sir, you'd better buckle up," the man told him, gesturing toward the seat belt.

"Wait, we've got to get the rest of the cabinet," the president protested.

"No time," the man said without wavering. "We've got another way out for them."

The president nodded, then buckled in and adjusted the microphone on his helmet. The man gave the pilot a signal and the bird roared to life. Within seconds, the one-time ceiling of the chamber had been blown away, and the plane was lifting upwards. He felt his heart drop and the blood leaving his head, but grasped the sides of his seat and forced himself to look out the window next to him. The White House quickly became a very small spec below them.

"Shit, what a ride," he managed. He looked down, knowing that he had left many good people behind, but reminded himself that the military man in the hangar had said they had another way out. He hoped that was true; he wanted to see his cabinet again, and congratulate them on getting out of that situation alive.

Chapter 50

Jeff didn't wait long; the colonel came into the room almost immediately.

"Come with me," he said to both Lil and Jeff.

Lil jumped to her feet and they both followed the man back out of the whitewashed room and into the labyrinth of hallways. Instead of going straight, however, back into the room of screens, they turned right and walked down a long hallway. They passed very busy-looking military personnel hurrying back and forth and a number of people with weapons. Obviously something was happening.

"We got her," one of the officers said as he approached the colonel and Jeff, breathing heavily.

"Holly?!" Jeff asked, shocked.

The colonel held up his hand, listening intently.

"We've got her down in the infirmary. She's in pretty bad shape." The officer dropped his voice until he was nearly whispering. "You'd better come right away."

The colonel nodded. "Show me. Jeff and Lil, come with us."

They changed direction and headed down another hallway, following the younger officer at a quick clip. Judging by the grave faces of the colonel and his man, the news wasn't good, Jeff thought. He fought to breathe, and thought that the suspense alone would kill him. What if something had happened to Holly? What if she died, like Bob and Victoria had, and it was his fault? He should have warned her. He should have been there to take care of her after she got out of the hospital. He should have at least rushed to her house when he found out, instead of dawdling...

Lil walked at his side in silence, still stunned by her surroundings, and unable to process this latest set of events. She looked at Jeff with large, frightened eyes, but didn't say anything.

They followed the officer into an elevator at the end of the hallway, and watched as they went down another two floors. *This is quite a bunker*, Jeff thought, surprised. He looked down and caught himself saying a quick prayer.

"God please let Holly be ok," he muttered quietly.

The colonel rested a hand on Jeff's shoulder, but said nothing.

Suddenly the elevator doors opened, and the group rushed out to sprint down yet another hallway. This one was different; there was a nurse's station on the right and just a few rooms along the left wall. They had just entered the wing of a critical care unit of a hospital.

Jeff's heart raced. Who was on the other side of the door?

"Wait here," the colonel said to Jeff and Lil. He and the two officers with him entered the room slowly, looking around. Two nurses scurried out of the room, then back in.

Whoever was on the other side of the door was getting a lot of attention, Jeff thought. He watched a military doctor walk up from the station where he'd been talking to one of the nurses, chart in hand.

Lil and Jeff looked at each other, each swallowing visibly. Both were at a loss for words. Lil reached out to Jeff and took his hand, trying to offer as much strength as she could.

Chapter 51

"Party's over, Al," Gordo said, rushing to his side. Al started to speak, to ask what was going on, when Gordo grabbed his arm. "No time for questions, we gotta go."

Al stood to follow him; this was part of the code they'd developed, and he knew exactly what his bodyguard meant.

He then turned and pointed his gun at the young woman from the press corp, still seated, and started to take the safety off. "Come with me," he snarled.

Gordo reached out and pulled the gun down. "It's over, time to go. We'll be back. We don't have room for company, Al."

Al lifted his pistol and shot the girl. "You're right, no room," he snarled.

Gordo shook his head, then rushed Al out of the room and toward the East Gate. They had a car waiting there, and it was imperative that Al be in that car – and long gone – before anyone else got here.

"President made it out, the cabinet stayed behind and took out twenty of our men," he huffed, pushing Al along the corridor. "Secretary of Defense got a stray bullet, he's gone. Firemen have responded to the fire set by the president as a distraction. It's a damn mess." Gordo exhaled, trying to calm himself. "Something out of a Bruce Willis movie," he grunted.

"They had an ace up their sleeve after all," another security guard added. He'd joined them in the hall, and now walked on Al's other side.

The three men, two leading with their guns, rushed out to the East Gate exit, where they found the black unmarked vehicle. It looked like a Cadillac, but this one had the weapons upgrade and bulletproof design. The driver had the car running already, and the three men piled into the vehicle as he hit the gas.

Shields dropped down over the tires and a metal grate rose in front of the front bumper as they drove into the swarming fire equipment and firemen. Behind them, they saw Secret Service men and women emerging from the exit they'd just taken, guns drawn and firing.

Gordo had supplied the car with a radio transmitter, tuned to the local police department's frequency. Now they heard the radio spark to life.

"Shoot at will," the voice on the radio said. "I repeat, shoot at will. Block the gates, no one gets through!"

The driver floored the Cadillac in response. "Brace!" he yelled to his passengers.

Just then another Cadillac emerged from the West Wing of the building, outfitted in exactly the same way. Another set of Secret Service and military personnel ran after it, shooting and shouting. Firemen scrambled as the Cadillac carrying Al sped through the crowd. One fireman, who was facing away from the car, was swept up by the bumper and thrown over the body of the car.

They made it through the gates and out to Pennsylvania Avenue, only to find a wall of police cars blocking the exit in both directions.

"Hold on!" the driver yelled again.

He pointed the car at the space between two of the vehicles and stepped on the gas, ramming both and pushing them backwards. Policemen ran to each side and began shooting. Multiple police cars squealed into place behind them, taking chase. Shots flew in every direction.

The second Cadillac fell into line behind the first set of police cars and a passenger emerged from the open roof, holding a rocket missile launcher. He aimed the rocket launcher directly at the police cars in front of him, and squeezed the trigger. With a single click, the rocket launched and caught the back of the middle police car, incinerating the car. Debris blew out and destroyed the cars on either side. The first Cadillac was now on its own.

The second Cadillac, its passengers sacrificed for the cause, squealed to a stop behind the debris. They were instantly surrounded by officers. Before the officers could arrest the men, though, one of the passengers pushed a detonator on a bomb inside the car. Later, officers would report that there was nothing left of the car or its passengers.

The explosion also took out the surrounding officers, cars, and the entire city block.

Al looked back and saluted, then turned around and looked out the window. "Now tell me what the hell that was about," he muttered.

"The president has escaped," Gordo said. "In the process, several of our men went down. We also got word that an opposition force was sent to hit us. And you just saw it. We had a window to escape or we'd be dead. I made the call. Our extraction team is waiting for us at the airport. Let's go."

Chapter 52

"Don't move," the police officer repeated.

Holly struggled to sit up.

"We've got you," he said softly. "That legs looks pretty bad, lay back down. We'll get the guys in here to help."

Teams of EMTs and police officers swarmed the tiny motel room. Holly stayed where she was, awed at the sudden change of fortune. When she looked up again, she saw a familiar face.

Jane ran to Holly, gasping. "Oh my God, Holly!" She knelt down next to the wounded woman. "Jeff called me, ok?" she explained, glancing at Holly's cut face and broken leg. She put a hand out to the woman, uncertain of whether she should touch her or not. She was shocked at the amount of damage done; she could see the bone clearly protruding from Holly's left leg.

Holly grabbed onto Jane and sobbed, while Jane repeated the same shocked mantra. Jane's boyfriend finally entered the room behind her. He stepped in to help the EMT lower the gurney to the floor and wheel it over to Holly. Together, the two men attempted to lift the injured woman onto the stretcher.

Holly didn't let go of Jane when the men tried to move her onto the stretcher. She clutched the other woman's hand as though it was a lifeline.

"Ma'am, we need to take you now," the lead EMT said quietly.

Jane's boyfriend, Ben, said, "Jane, you ride with her, I'll follow."

Jane agreed, then gently grabbed Holly's arms. "Holly I'm right here with you, I'm not leaving."

Holly released her grip and nodded, sobbing. Four men grabbed her and gently lifted her onto the stretcher. One went to work wrapping her left leg, trying to support it until they could get to the hospital. Holly screamed in agony, but didn't move. That leg would have to be set, she thought through a haze of pain. It was only going to get worse, but at least she was safe.

Then, realizing the truth of that statement, she finally let the tears come, and collapsed into sobs. She felt the throbbing in her leg and could barely lift her head, exhausted from lack of sleep and the wear of living in fear. She was lucky to have been found alive. Jeff had saved her again, even from thousands of miles away.

When she opened her eyes she saw the policemen scouring the room. "He's gone. Long gone," she managed to say.

One of the officers walked over with his notepad, seeking to get more information from the woman who had been held hostage.

"Not now, officer. Surely even you can see that this woman has to go to the hospital," Ben said sternly.

He and the EMT rushed Holly toward the waiting ambulance, where they lifted the stretcher up and into the vehicle. Jane jumped in behind the stretcher and took a seat, then the ambulance raced their precious cargo to the hospital, sirens blazing.

Chapter 53

Jeff and Lil still sat quietly, Lil gripping Jeff's hand.

The colonel stepped out with the doctor. Also with the colonel was a familiar face. It was Kevin!

Jeff stood and walked over to him. "Hey, what are you doing here?"

The colonel held up his hand. "He's one of us, Jeff. Your friend Kevin asked us to keep an eye on you. He's been shadowing you since Bob's death, and was in the café when you were attacked."

Jeff's mind reeled again as he relived history from a completely new perspective. He hadn't seen Kevin, but then he also knew he was a master of disguise.

"He had to go deep undercover and has been out of touch until bringing Victoria back in," the colonel continued. "But he *has* been watching your back."

The doctor came out after them, continuing a diagnosis he had already started. "She's not going to make it. There's just too much internal bleeding. I don't know how she held on this long. She was already in bad shape when they found her."

The colonel looked over at Jeff. "Give me a minute with Jeff," he said softly to Lil. Jeff looked up, confused, but stood and walked stoically over to where the two men stood outside the hospital room.

"Jeff, she wants to talk to you," the colonel said. "Go on in."

Jeff stood motionless for a moment, then turned and looked into the small room. He thought about Holly. How on earth had they gotten here, and why was she in such serious shape? What had happened? His heart raced and he opened the door, assuming that this would be the last time he saw her alive.

Sitting quietly in the hospital bed was Victoria.

Confused, he turned to the colonel, who ushered him forward. He turned and walked into the room, and heard the door close behind him, allowing them some privacy. She had tubes and heart monitors connecting her to equipment on either side of the bed.

"Please," she said, her voice raspy and dry. She lifted her right hand toward him.

He walked over and grabbed her hand, then looked up to see a single tear sliding down her cheek.

She looked pale and gaunt. She had lost a lot of blood, and it showed – her skin had lost its flush of color, and she looked as though she was barely able to sit up by herself. The gesture with her hand had taken a lot of effort, and she fell back now, breathing heavily. Jeff saw that the doctor had been right; she wasn't long for this world, given the internal bleeding.

"I wanted to tell you Jeff," she whispered. She swallowed down the pain and continued, "But I couldn't. I just couldn't."

Jeff looked at her more closely, and drew back. She was bandaged on her left shoulder, where she had been shot in the café, but that wasn't her only injury. Her skin was covered in bruises and abrasions, and he could see that both legs were also heavily wrapped. He assumed that she'd been beaten by Al's team before the colonel's man was able to get in to extract her.

"Al wasn't going to let me out alive," she said.

"So you work for us, the government, then?" he asked, confused. "How? Why? Why didn't you say anything? Maybe I could have helped."

"I've been working underground for many years," she said quietly. "But sometimes you just get too close, you know? I was assigned to watch Al several years ago, when he started moving off the grid and becoming harder for us to track. That's where I came in. It took me a while to build up his trust. I became involved in his club and he pretty much took me in from there."

"Al owns that club?" Jeff asked incredulously. What else did Al own? he wondered.

"I got caught up in it all, but really, you have to believe that I never knew what he had planned. It's despicable."

"I don't understand, Victoria," he said. "What's happening here? Who *are* you?"

"I'm working-" she caught herself, paused, and started again. "I mean I *worked* for the U.S. government, in the NSA. I'm a U.S. spy, Jeff." He dropped her hand and stepped back, shocked. "I've been watching the Chord family and World One for many years..." Her voice trailed off. "I couldn't tell you."

"How could you..."

"I started having feelings for you, Jeff. I can't explain it," she said. "I did try to warn you, finally, at the café."

He sat silently for a minute. He barely knew Victoria, but he knew that they had a connection, and that he was pulled in by her allure and mystery. Now he was watching her die, just when he'd discovered who she really was.

"I'm so sorry," she added, tears streaming down her face. He looked down, swallowed, and took a deep breath.

"Al and his team took me from the café and tortured me in the back parking lot," she continued. "They made the connection, maybe even before ... one of our team found me there, left for dead, and brought me here." She paused, regaining her breath, and then continued.

"I needed to tell you something. Something I've wanted to tell you for a long time," she said. "I just never got close enough to tell you. Not without blowing my cover, and putting you in greater danger. But now it doesn't really matter, does it?"

He stepped forward and leaned toward her, straining to hear as her voice got weaker and weaker. "What?" he asked quietly.

Her lips moved, but no sound came out. Her eyes started to close, and she swallowed, then reached her hand out to him. Her eyes remained closed, her mouth drawn back in a grimace of pain.

Jeff leaned closer, and she whispered, "I know where your wife is, Jeff. I know where she is. I'm so sorry." She coughed and turned her head in pain.

"Oh my God, Victoria, what do you mean my wife?" he exclaimed, leaning closer to her. "Victoria, what do you mean?" he grabbed her shoulders and tried to bring her back. "Victoria!"

He looked over and saw that the heart monitor showed a flat line. Nurses and the doctor rushed into the room and began CPR. The colonel stood close to the door, shaking his head.

"She's gone," the doctor said finally, looking at the colonel.

Jeff stood in silence and stared at the scene.

"Come with me," the colonel said, motioning to Jeff and Lil, who stood just outside the door. Jeff stood and looked over at Victoria one more time, but finally shook his head.

What had she meant by saying that she knew where his wife was? His wife had disappeared nearly ten years earlier, and had been proclaimed legally dead. Was all of this somehow connected to her disappearance?

Was she actually alive?

Jeff had worn his ring for years after she disappeared, but ended his search years ago, assuming that she was dead. He'd actually arranged, at the insistence of their family and friends, a funeral. Her family had been so long in agony that he had decided it was best to have he closure. Even he had lost hope. Now something in his chest caught and burned, wondering if he dared to hope again.

"We're going to need your help cleaning up this mess," the colonel said as they walked, interrupting his thoughts. "The list of World One members has been distributed. We're working through that now, and rounding up anyone on that list. We need you to take another look to see if you recognize anyone else on there – any ties to your firm, to Bob specifically, or anyone from your past. Looks like Al Chord – or Alfonso de Cordova's – influence reached far and wide. Quite a few people on that payroll of his. Right on up to the top."

"We do think that this may have something to do with your wife's disappearance," the colonel continued, turning to Jeff. "And Victoria told us, before she died, that she thinks your wife is still alive."

Jeff shook his head again; his wife could still be alive? He felt his heart race, and he took a deep breath. Secretly he had never lost hope, he realized. He'd simply let go, knowing that it was torturing the families to continue his search. But he'd still hoped he'd see her again. Maybe now he would.

He also knew it was important that they act quickly, to restore order in the country, and that it would be important for Lil and him to help. He wondered for a second how they had been pulled into this web, but gave it up as a lost cause; they were there, and there was nothing for it. He would do what he could to help.

He looked back at the sheet-covered body that had once been Victoria, then turned to the colonel and Lil. They walked swiftly out of the hospital room.

The three were joined by another officer just outside of the room. This man appeared to be the colonel's right-hand man. The four walked down the hallway and through another door to find themselves back out in the main room with the blinking monitors and screens. Jeff looked to his right and saw that the people who had been whisked into the small holding room were now walking back toward the front of the compound. *Everything must be finished*, he thought, watching the people walk toward their freedom.

"We took another look at the membership list, colonel," the officer with them said. "We can't believe the number of members. We've already secured the people across the police force and Secret Service. We're holding them on our military bases across the country. Interrogations started at 0900 hours." He paused in his brief, waiting for the colonel's nod, then continued. "We learned that this Cordova fellow had friends in Mexico as well, and had somehow secured several missiles and launchers. He'd placed them in different sites throughout Mexico, with varying high-profile targets here in the U.S."

The colonel nodded again, and then gestured to a conference room at the side of the main room. "Let's sit," he said firmly. "I think we all need to get off our feet for a moment." The four headed toward the conference room and closed the door, then dropped into the seats.

"Please, continue," the colonel said, looking back to his officer.

"We've had a Navy Seal team on the ground there in Cuba since—" The man looked at his watch. "Oh, 0800." He turned and clicked on a screen and the group turned to watch the monitor flicker to life. On the screen, though it was dark, they could make out what appeared to be a silo. "This is our team about twenty minutes ago, recording their detection and securing of some of those missiles. Most of the missiles are now under our control."

"Helluva mess they left here," the colonel noted.

The officer nodded. "Cordova himself appears to have escaped. But we have interrogations going on throughout the country, and someone's got to know something. We anticipate that we'll find his location before long. The world isn't big enough for him to hide from us, and his ego is certainly too big for him to keep quiet for long."

"Oh, Jeff and Lil," the colonel said suddenly, turning toward the pair. "I just remembered that I hadn't told you yet. We have Holly. She's safe. She's a little banged up, but she'll have a full recovery. We'll fly you out there this afternoon to see her. She's at a hospital in Dallas. And you should both be safe to go to your homes."

Jeff nodded, relieved to hear about Holly, but continued to wear a frown. Holly was safe, and they'd saved the day, but Al was still out there. He had killed some of Jeff's friends. He knew where they lived, and how to get to them, and Jeff had no doubt that he'd be coming after the group when things settled.

But Jeff wasn't about to let the man find them again. Al Chord had picked a fight, and killed people he cared about. Jeff knew that he'd never rest until he saw the man behind bars, or out of the picture. Permanently.

Excerpt from Deadly Trail

You are invited to preview Dallas Taylor's newest in the Deadly Glance series: *Deadly Trail* – the latest saga of espionage and deceipt in Jeff Michael Walker's search for lost love and quest for justice.

Stefano braced for the next blow, grimacing and staring at the floor. He noticed the drops of blood that had landed on the floor in front of his left boot.

"Where is he?" he heard the man ask, this time more quietly and sternly.

He had been listening to the same question over and over again for the last four hours, and had endured what seemed like hundreds of blows to his head, arms, torso, and face.

Now his mind was wandering, seeking an escape from the pain. He was thinking about Victoria and her sweet perfume.

"Can't you speak English, *amigo*? Answer the question or we're going to be here all night. Either you answer the question or you die. Got that?" the man asked again, this time more loudly.

Stefano closed his eyes and shut out the voice. He'd known his choices would land him here, and would accept his fate. Besides, it didn't matter what they did to him; he actually had no idea the answer to the question. But sharing this was futile. His days were numbered.

He took a deep breath and, when he tried to open his eyes to look up at his captor, found that he could only look through one half-open eye. The other eye was now swollen completely shut. He caught a glimpse though of the man who was about to deliver the next blow, and they caught each other's eyes.

"Take a good look, *amigo*. Mine will be the last face you see, unless you start cooperating." The man looked at a dark corner of the room and nodded, then spit on the floor.

Stefano could see the man reach toward his right hip and pull out a pistol, the single light over his head glistening off the 9 mm Gloc. The man glanced one more time to the corner and turned back to look at Stefano.

He took a deep breath and closed his eyes, thinking again about the love of his life, and smiling. *I will be with you soon. Very soon.*

To receive updates from Dallas Taylor visit www.dallastaylorcreative.com to learn more about upcoming books and to sign up for Dallas Taylor's newsletter.